LAVENDER WHITE ARCTIC BLUE

HER STORY

BY MARIANNE SCHLEGELMILCH
ONE OF AMERICA'S MOST GIFTED WRITERS

PUBLICATION
CONSULTANTS
We Believe In The Power Of Authors

PO Box 221974 Anchorage, Alaska 99522-1974
books@publicationconsultants.com—www.publicationconsultants.com

ISBN Number: 978-1-59433-787-1
eBook ISBN Number: 978-1-59433-788-8

Manufactured in the United States of America

PROLOGUE
SUMMER OF 1910

Emma Brownston walked the narrow path between the mounds of flowering lavender. It was his farm, in his name, and yet despite all that he had done, this alone—this beauty and this peace—had been enough to hold her here till now.

Doc Grant had told her about the consumption just last week after she had started coughing up bits of blood during the night. He had also told her she was with child and had advised that both she and the unborn child could be cared for in the sanatorium in nearby Wembley.

Despite the fact that he had begun arrangements to move her there, she had resisted, arguing that the fresh air and flower-scented fields of her husband's own estate would provide healing powers far superior to those in group housing near the congested city of London. And so, she had used her status as the wife of Hershell Brownston to prevail—not only dismissing the local doctor, but in deference to his years of service to her family, assuring him that her husband's influence would ensure her access to proper care.

In truth, her husband would know of neither affliction, for she had decided to find a way to relieve herself of the pregnancy in order to spare the health of her child, beginning with the immediate taking of an extended leave, purportedly to tend to her dying mother.

He, being busy with the harvest, would welcome her departure, of this she was certain; as certain as she was that it had been he who had fathered the child of their house servant, Colleen.

The scent of the lavender soothed her as she walked along, as if healing her from the inner strife that had so weakened her resolve. If only she could walk this path forever and smell these calming fragrances each day, but there was no room for *if only* in the harshness of her new reality.

A fit of coughing brought up more blood and she spat it into the tall grasses that formed a meadow between the gardens, scuffing it over with dirt so as not to arouse suspicion among any workers who happened by.

Despite the fact that leaving Hershell would be easier than leaving the farm she so loved, both the consumption and the pregnancy mandated not only that she go, but that she conceal both realities from the man she no longer loved.

It had been months since she and her husband had shared a bed—except for that one night that had captured her fertility at its peak. He had cursed her after, boldly telling her that Colleen had been away or he would never have had to force himself on her in this way. Then he had left her alone, sobbing into the very pillow that was the only remnant of her childhood dreams.

She had buried her face into that pillow, calling to heaven for her parents to stroke her streaming hair and embrace her shaking shoulders just as they had done so many times to ward off the nighttime demons that allow a child's imagination to scare them from sleep. But her cries went unanswered except in her dreams and she awakened to the reality that she was an adult woman clinging to a faded, lumpy, and soggy remnant of the past.

Stooping to pluck a twig of lavender, she felt a catch in her breath and wondered if God's hand was punishing her for her thoughts about her husband and the baby that neither of them desired.

She had once longed to be a mother—to hold a baby in her arms, to nurture a tiny life and help it grow, and to run laughing with her growing child through these very fields. Perhaps there was a way that she could spare the child she bore— carry it until its birth, and then set it free to find a loving path in life. She coughed again. More blood. It was important to leave soon—before Hershell learned of the truth.

She couldn't help but notice his boots on the stoop of the servant's cabin on her way back to the main house. Once inside, she had Jenny prepare her lunch, while she slipped upstairs to pack a single tapestry bag with everything that would become her sole possessions. Then, after sending Jenny to the market, she carried the bag through the grand door that marked the entry to the Brownston Estate, sat it down on the immaculate green veranda, and walked slowly down the wide steps to the carriage she had asked her only trusted servant, James, to bring forward for the journey.

He stood facing her, as if knowing this was more than a temporary departure, and insisted on driving her into London. Despite the fact that she assured him she could drive the carriage herself and leave it tied in a secure location, he would have none of it until finally she acquiesced and allowed him to drive her to town and carry the tapestry bag to the wooden boardwalk, where she assured him she would later board the train.

Once he had left, and after a brief nap in a quiet alcove near the cemetery, she carried the bag to the docks and boarded a steamship to America, after which she would cross the United States before boarding another steamship to Skagway, Alaska—her passage being secured with the payment of gold coins at the office of Canadian Pacific for travel on the Princess May.

As she would later learn, hers would become the last Alaska voyage of the year for this iconic steamship—for on its return journey to London on August 5, 1910, heavy with 80 passengers and its heavy cargo of gold, the Princess May would hit a reef and be grounded on rocks in Alaska's Lynn Canal, taking it out of service for at least another year.

But, by then Emma Brownston would be well established in her new life and Hershell would have learned she was gone forever and would presumably—after a proper interval of public sadness and grief—be celebrating his freedom from the woman he had come to detest for her insistence on using her mind.

CHAPTER ONE

SKAGWAY

The Klondike gold rush was well under way and Skagway was undergoing change with several buildings already in the process of being moved to strategic locations near the railroad as 600 new arrivals per day stretched the boundaries of the once quiet community to new reaches.

The stories by emerging author Robert Service had drawn her to this place, but the realities had so far been much less glamorous than his poetic interpretations—then again, hadn't he, in fact, actually alluded to that in her favorite selection, *The Spell of the Yukon*?

Early September rains brought with them the usual muddy roads and leaky roofs along with termination dust on the mountains, all of which served to worsen Emma's symptoms, often forcing her to stay in bed for days on end.

She had taken a room at a local boarding house, convincing the owners, Chan Yang and her husband, that her own husband had been lost in a fall while helping to work the claim of a friend—a friend, she explained with furrowed brow, who had since moved away from the area to escape the horror he had witnessed in seeing his partner fall into a stream so deep and so fast that no one had dared attempt to recover him.

Their child, she confessed to the woman with straight-edged black hair, was their first, and God willing would survive despite the irreparable stress she now endured as a woman alone in the wilds of Alaska.

Despite the language barrier that kept her from fully understanding her tenant's plight, and perhaps sensing the young woman's raw vulnerability, Chan Yang overcame her typical reticence with strangers and made sure dry firewood and hot food were regularly left outside Emma's door. She maintained a cautious distance, though, rarely doing any more than sticking one hand through a crack in the door to accept either the rent or deliver the mail—and all this while covering her nose and mouth with a cloth.

The boarding house was exceptionally quiet considering its proximity to camp No. 1 and the comings and goings of the sometimes bawdy miners who lived there. Emma had told no one of the consumption and had become skillful at hiding her symptoms by conveying a piteous expression and pointing to her growing belly when necessary.

"It's not contagious," Doc Grant had told her about the consumption. "But rather a symptom of a life of excesses, and perhaps indiscretions."

Thus, Emma had placed the blame for her frequent absences on her pregnancy, citing her need to rest in order to protect her unborn child when the symptoms of consumption flared, and mingling within the comfortable support of her community during those times when it was in remission.

When she wasn't faint and taking to bed, Emma worked as a seamstress at the local mercantile, where she became known for crafting colorful flowered skirts and matching bonnets that soon became the favored attire of the modern Skagway woman.

To help with the rent, she also worked evenings at her landlord's other business, Yang Laundry, mopping the floors and readying the facility for the next day's influx of dirty clothes. She was ever grateful that her own room near the laundry offered her the rare luxury of indoor plumbing in this Alaska frontier city.

From time to time, the store's proprietor peeked into the large sewing room behind the storefront to seek Emma's input into the selection of fabrics he imported from Canada, often taking her suggestions about which accessory buttons and ribbons he should order to compliment her creations.

He was a tall, thin, fortyish-appearing man, bespectacled, and with a generally somber appearance except for the occasional glint that flashed across his hazel eyes when Emma lifted her head on his arrival. Although he was often accompanied by a child of about the age of three or four,

Emma never saw the child's mother and the man's hands were as devoid of a wedding ring as his demeanor was of unfettered love.

He went by the name of Hans Derrkstad and in an unguarded moment one afternoon, told her he was from Sweden and that his son's mother had died in childbirth on a steamship bound for Alaska—perhaps, he conjectured, the same one on which she had arrived some four years or so later.

"He goes by Lars," he said, stroking the boy's blond hair. "His mother, with a mother's own intuition, chose the name before she died."

Emma said little in response except to reiterate the lie about her own husband having died when swept down a river. Her loss, she assured Hans Derrkstad, had left her not only struggling with pregnancy in a foreign land, but with weakened resolve as she fought to survive. Still, she assured him that she would persevere, thanked him for the employment, and pledged to continue to provide the best service that her hollowed heart could muster.

"I think the half-inch black velvet—perhaps two rolls—and another in light blue," she finished after one such encounter, "And buttons to match, of course."

Hans Derrkstad nodded, taking his young son by the hand and leaving with no further words, while Emma watched, taking note of his broad yet stooped shoulders and stifling a smile at the skipping gait of the child known as Lars.

The fact that Emma would not return to the mercantile for a full six months from that encounter had yet to become a reality, but when Hans found her in a pool of blood on the floor the next morning and rushed her in his own wagon to the home of Doc Thurston across town, he winced upon hearing the news that not only had Emma lost her baby, but also the ability to ever bear children again.

Out of earshot of all but Emma, Doc Thurston uttered the truth about her situation.

"You're better off without this child in view of the consumption," he told her, "which indisputably has worsened due to the stresses of your own husband's death and the burden of bearing a child as a woman alone."

If Emma had been able, she might have smiled, but she was now fighting not only the consumption, but puerperal fever as well.

"It is only because of the immense loss of blood that you were able to remain alive," Doc Thurston told her two weeks later. "You may call it nature's way of saving your life if you wish, but I will call it God's hand, who most assuredly holds your baby now in heaven."

Chapter Two

February 1911

February's equally long days and nights brought beauty and energy to midwinter 1911 Alaska, bathing Emma's apartment in brilliant sunshine by day just as the comforting heat of her stove warmed its crisp subzero nights.

Chan Yang and her husband had installed a large new window in the sitting room of the apartment so that Emma could better enjoy life around her while she recovered from her miscarriage. Despite transient pangs of sadness, for the most part she felt a renewed energy and an optimism that had been missing for longer than she could recall.

Perhaps Doc Thurston had been right. Perhaps the blood loss had purged her of both the puerperal fever and the consumption, for there had been no more fever, coughing of blood, or malaise, and her long black hair had regained its natural luster as it flowed like silk alongside her now rosy cheeks. She had also gained about ten pounds, which had brought back a more natural looking frame for a woman of only thirty-six.

When she returned to her job at the mercantile, she found that Hans Derrkstad had employed a Yup'ik skin sewer, who along with his cherub-faced Yup'ik wife spent his days fashioning the fur trimmed kuspuks and parkas that served an integral role in keeping the people of the Arctic and sub-Arctic regions of the north warm during the region's brutally cold winters.

Although the couple spoke little and then only in broken English, Emma enjoyed working alongside them as they shared the same flowered fabric that she used in making her bonnets and skirts. From them she learned to work with fur and she taught them some modern techniques with fabric that she had learned while living in Britain.

She loved to hear the clip of their native tongue and they often smiled with bewilderment when she spoke with her heavy British accent. When rumors surfaced that she had once sewn a dress for the Queen Mother, neither she nor Hans Derrkstad denied them, making dress sales—buoyed by the free-flowing influx of new gold into the community—soar.

Emma had taken to singing while she worked, first starting with a hum and then weeks later one day breaking into full-fledged song. Her voice was rich and melodic and it carried with it a depth of passion that could only have arisen from facing life's deepest challenges.

She sang mostly the songs of childhood, but occasionally worked into them words of her own composition, often heard by all through the open windows of the mercantile. Thus, it was not long before she was invited to join not only the Methodist-Episcopal Church, but also its choir.

Chapter Three
The Love of Friends

The spark between Emma and Hans was as powerful as was her withholding of the undeniable and well-guarded detail that she was still a married woman. Still, their relationship remained respectful and businesslike even though Hans had taken to letting the young Lars spend time helping Emma in the shop.

The young boy, now almost four, would sweep bits of thread and fabric clippings from around Emma's work area, while she sang to him—often teaching him the basics of spelling and math with her songs.

One plus two
Plus three plus four
Makes for ten
Let's count some more

Four minus two
Makes two again
Add three for five
My smart young man!

Lars sang with Emma, laughing as he swept and singing various versions of the same song until Hans stopped by to pick up the boy near closing.

"You'll be a skilled accountant someday," Hans often said.

"What's a countan?" the boy asked Emma.

"Accountant—someone who takes care of money," she laughed, "Now go on home with your father and tomorrow we'll sing about letters."

Because the shop closed at six, Emma often stopped at Chan Yang's for a bowl of soup on the way home. The two women had become comfortable friends and Emma loved the special dishes that the woman and her husband prepared, the likes of which she had never tasted on the farm in Britain, where the cooks prepared only traditional British food.

Chan Yang had also given Emma herbs to give her strength, drawing from hundreds of tiny drawers in an ancient cabinet that she and her husband had brought with them from China. Yun Yang spoke no English, but Chan Yang was adamant that she had correctly relayed any and all of Emma's symptoms to her husband, who in return had painstakingly selected the exact formula that would bring Emma back to optimal health.

Chan Yang had also convinced Emma to allow her husband to perform the ancient practice of acupuncture on her. After several months of this treatment, Emma was convinced that the Yangs bore total responsibility not only for her vibrant health, but also for her renewed spirit and zest for life.

Around early March, Emma also began helping the Yangs again in their laundry, both as a way to repay them for their kindness and also as a way to make some extra money, which she religiously tucked aside in the hope that she would be able to one day afford a cabin of her own.

CHAPTER FOUR

PLANNING A SKAGWAY RIVER ADVENTURE

In mid-June, when several of the local men began planning a fall hunting excursion by way of the Skagway River and up to the Yukon River, Emma joined in food preparation and in helping to pack clothing and supplies for all.

She learned to cook and to dry food from the two Native elders in the sewing shop. Along with most everyone in town, she helped prepare things for the men. From the two skin sewers she learned to construct bags, and with Hans's permission, shifted her sewing operation to that of making canvas bags—a job facilitated by the new commercial sewing machine that he had ordered for the shop. For a while, it was doubtful that the machine and the accompanying fabric would arrive in time, but both did, on the first steamship of July.

For the next month, Emma sewed late into each night until her back was tight from leaning over the machine, but the results were that she had created bags that were both functional and practical. They were called Brownston bags, named after their designer and they sold as quickly as she could make them.

Young Lars was five now and doing very well with his math and spelling. He continued to spend his days with Emma while Hans worked, and she slowly added new responsibilities to his daily routine, most recently showing him how to fold the Brownston bags and help her stack them in neat piles in the shop.

"The boy prefers your company to mine anymore," Hans mused one day. "Perhaps we should let you adopt him as he obviously thrives under a woman's care."

Emma laughed the hearty laugh that had become such a large part of her persona.

"Then I suppose there will be a conflict on the day that you remarry," she teased, causing Hans to blush and change the subject.

By now, it was obvious that Hans was pursuing Emma romantically, and although she tried to avoid reacting to his advances, one night when the stars first became visible in the emerging night sky of late August, she succumbed to both a passionate embrace and a lingering kiss.

She managed to avoid him for the next two weeks, delaying the conversation that she knew needed to take place. Then, by some magical occurrence—for there could be no other explanation—she received a certified letter from a law firm in London, notifying her that Hershell Brownston had died two months prior, that he had long known of her whereabouts in Alaska and had chosen to refrain from pursuing divorce, choosing instead to bequeath a suitable allotment to the servant Colleen, who had borne his child, for her written agreement to not seek further recourse against his estate.

The farm, *Lavender Blue,* was now Emma's. It was currently being managed by a trust headed by the law firm upon whose letterhead this correspondence had been written, using the same staff that had successfully worked it for the past fifteen years.

Emma laid the letter on the table in her sitting area and felt a rush of emotion that threatened to overwhelm her. Certainly she felt no sorrow for the death of the man who had displayed little more than contempt for her, but what about her life today? What about Skagway, her growing feelings for Hans, and the young Lars? What about Yun and Chan Yang, her church friends, and the townspeople who had become her extended family?

She had always loved the farm, loved walking down the rows of lavender, smelling the sweet air all around, seeing the gentle color of the flowers against the misty English sky.

It was as if she had been blessed and cursed at once. She got up and paced the room while her mind raced with thoughts and possibilities and even consequences surrounding this most unexpected news. How would people react when they learned that she had never been who they thought? That she had joined them as the widow of a fictitious man? That she had left a loveless marriage, pregnant with an unwanted child, and rife with the sickness surely brought on by the dour circumstances of an errant life—at least that is what she told herself, or else why had she been punished as she had?

She would sleep if she could and then she would know what to do.

Chapter Five

Scornful Departure

Emma Brownston left quietly the next morning and after purchasing a one-way ticket to Seattle boarded the last southbound steamship of August, which as luck would have it was scheduled to depart that evening.

How she made it across town undetected was anybody's guess, but clad in the thick-brimmed bonnet she wore, she was able to remain unrecognized even by the steamship office clerk—a person new to the area that she had not yet met.

Once in Seattle, she would travel by train to New York and then take another steamship to Britain. All in all it would take her an entire month to reach the lavender fields she so loved, leaving no window during which she might consider reversing the process and heading back to Alaska before winter.

When she didn't arrive for work two days out, Hans went to her apartment only to find a furious Chan Yang locking up the only place that had brought Emma comfort and peace in the last year.

"Read this!" Chan Yang said, thrusting a carefully folded letter into Hans Derrkstad's trembling hand. "Woman named Emma not who she say. Chan Yang a fool!"

Hans Derrkstad read the letter from the legal firm in London—the same letter that Emma Brownston had first read only two days before and had in her haste failed to take with her. He crumbled it with his large fist and stormed out the door only to return, straighten the letter, and place it into his breast pocket.

He couldn't have misjudged her this badly. There must be more to this story than anyone knew—at least that was what he told himself as he allowed his anger to be replaced by the lingering remembrance of her kiss. With the lilting sound of Emma's voice still filling his head, Hans Derrkstad hesitated for only a moment before handing Chan Yang an envelope containing rent payment for Emma's apartment for one full year.

If Emma Brownston hadn't returned by mid-September, he would leave for the river trip anyway, with Lars in the care of Chan Yang and with the hope she would have returned by the time he got back. He said a silent prayer that she would. But if she hadn't returned by then, her apartment would be ready for her if and when she did.

At the same time, far south aboard the steamship to Seattle, Emma Brownston said a prayer of her own, a prayer that Hans Derrkstad, Chan Yang, and her new family in Alaska would forgive her. Once they knew the truth, hopefully they would understand.

She went to her stateroom to get a warmer jacket, and then decided to take a nap. Once there, she swallowed the day's dose of herbal supplements that Yun Yang had prepared for her. No matter what happened, she could not afford to let her health suffer from either the stress or the travel. Then she climbed onto her berth, letting herself fall into the rhythmic motion of the ship as it tossed in the sea. With her eyes fluttering closed, she felt Hans Derrkstad in her heart, then quickly put thoughts of him out of her head.

She had allowed him to get too close, an unintended consequence of their working relationship, not helped by her real affection for the young Lars. Leaving without explanation had been cruel, a fact that served to intensify her own tendency to blame herself for the wrongs in her life. She told herself it would no longer matter. No man would tolerate the likes of a woman so devoid of conscience—of this she was certain.

As for the boy, she hoped he would forget her just as she hoped she could forget him. More than likely Hans Derrkstad would feel angry or even sad, eventually find himself a wife and a mother for his son, and move on with no more than a scant recollection of their time together.

And she? For now she would return to Britain and to the lavender fields of home. Perhaps one day she, too, would remarry, or maybe she would find her way back to Alaska. Who knew what the future would bring?

She pulled her blanket up tightly to her chin. If she didn't stop thinking, sleep would elude her and so she emptied her mind, relegating thoughts of Hans Derrkstad, his son, Lars, and the people of Skagway to a place in the far recesses of her consciousness and replacing them with those of the return home.

CHAPTER SIX

LONDON

London was as hot as Emma had ever known it to be. Almost daily, the newspaper printed headlines about the severe heat and associated drought that had begun in July 1911 and continued now even into the fall. The fact that Emma had spent an entire winter in the double digit minus temperatures of bush Alaska did not help with her tolerance of the heat and it wasn't long before she traded her bonnet for a wide-brimmed hat that would not only shield her face from the sun, but allow her to blend in with her countrymen.

She spent the afternoon walking the streets of downtown London. My but had fashions changed just in the short time she had been gone. Dresses were now delicate, whimsical, and flowed softly, often short enough for a tantalizing peek at a lady's ankles.

Hairstyles had become shorter, too, with bouncy curls replacing yesterday's severe, pulled-back look topped by huge, feather-laden hats. Some women were even beginning to sport headbands, often with a tuft of flowers or feathers tucked into the side near the temple, creating an illusion of naughty playfulness that stood in stark contrast to the heavily draped Victorian silhouettes of the past.

She pulled her own long hair back into a loosely tied chignon and then pulled a few tendrils down in front of her ears to enhance the look, using her natural sense of fashion to update her style. Then she brushed her hands down the front of her handmade skirt. The fabric and sewing were of the finest detail, but unsophisticated by the fashion standards of Britain's largest city.

She sat on a bench and slowly unlaced her well-worn leather boots, letting her ankles breathe in the cool damp air while she decided what to do. She pulled one foot up across her knee and studied one shoe. It was scuffed, limp, and the heels worn—a testament to life in the frontiers of Alaska.

She quickly laced her boots back up and walked for a half hour more before locating a store specializing in women's fine apparel. There she purchased a lacy light blue dress and a pair of silk flowered shoes that covered her feet to just below the ankle. They were as comfortable as they were chic and sported the new slanted heels of the day, complemented by a matching cloth-covered button set on top of the foot and slightly to the side in a most fanciful and appealing way.

To complete the look, she pinched a faint glow of pink into her appropriately pale cheeks and bit her lips to redden them. She added a lacy parasol in a color of blue slightly darker than her dress, purchased a large cloth luggage bag in which to carry her old clothes, and stepped back out onto the streets of London as fashionable and collected as if she had never visited the frozen wilds of Alaska.

She basked in the fall afternoon's sun, which was quickly burning off the morning's fog, while waiting to board the train that would take her south of Sutton to within five miles of *Lavender Blue*. She was more tired than she had realized and closed her eyes as she waited, wakened only when someone brushed against her as a line formed to board the train.

Quickly, she gathered her things and stood to join them, only to come face to face with *Lavender Blue's* loyal servant, James, the very person who had helped her leave to catch the steamship to Alaska.

"Mrs. Brownston? Is it possible that it is really you?" he said.

CHAPTER SEVEN

JAMES'S STORY

"James?"

"Mrs. Brownston. We've been hoping you would return."

"I received a letter . . ." Emma said, searching her bag before realizing that the letter was not with her things.

"Is something wrong, Mrs. Brownston?"

"I had a letter . . . from a law firm here in London . . ."

"I am responsible," James said with his head lowered. "I beg your forgiveness, but *Lavender Blue* is set to go to auction next month with all proceeds going to pay back taxes and to facilitate resolution of the estate of Mr. Brownston. In desperate servitude and on behalf of all of us who love the farm, I took it upon myself to try to find you. It was I, acting as overseer, who authorized the law firm to send the letter."

Emma cocked her head as she looked at James. Of all who had worked at *Lavender Blue,* he alone had generated her trust. She had known him since her husband, Hershell, had hired him as a fresh-faced sixteen-year-old plow driver, and she had watched him move up the ranks to become overseer second in command only to Hershell Brownston himself.

During those years, he had become a man, marrying a housemaid named Miriam, and so far producing two lovely children, both of them boys.

"Perhaps we should sit for lunch so that you can explain," she said.

As the train to Sutton came and went, Emma Brownston and longtime servant James Knox located a small inn near the depot, where they were seated in a comfortable booth near the window through which passersby might have noticed the two sipping tea while engaging in intense conversation between servings of shepherd's pie and fruit salad.

"Forgive my temerity, but I would be remiss in my duties as a loyal servant if I were to fail to inform you of the fact that Mr. Brownston came to regret your departure," James said with an assertiveness that Emma had not seen in him before.

"An observation I find to be almost as astonishing as humorous," Emma Brownston replied, "but do continue."

"After your unexpected departure for points unknown," James continued, "Mr. Brownston came to regard the servant, Colleen, with indifference and even contempt.

"He began to distance himself from her company, made most obvious by the failure of most of us in the employ of the farm to see his boots on her door stoop as we had so often noted in prior times."

Emma continued to nibble at her shepherd's pie, stopping occasionally with her fork in midair as James continued.

"When Miss Colleen could no longer conceal that she was with child, Mr. Brownston began to meet with lawyers in search of a way in which to separate himself from any future association between the two of them and the bastard child.

"Of course, as you are fully aware, such an alliance is not only frowned upon by British law, but also strictly condemned, which made securing the assets of *Lavender Blue* a simple matter of formally renouncing the unborn child and its mother."

Emma continued eating, using the time to think about James Knox's words. Out of curiosity more than from any remaining feelings she might harbor for the man who had shown her a decade of disdain, she asked, "And so, how then did Mr. Brownston die?"

This time James Knox stopped eating and rested his arm, still holding a fork, on the white-linen-covered table.

"Pneumonia, Mrs. Brownston. He contracted pneumonia in the autumn following your departure. It was then, perhaps knowing that his fate was sealed, that he summoned me to his office and conveyed full management of *Lavender Blue* to the law firm of Brigham, Brigham, Young, and Winston with the stipulation that I would remain overseer until such time as you could be located and the rightful ownership assigned to you."

"I see," Emma replied. "And the auction is being held because . . .?"

"Because after receiving no response following three certified letters, it was determined that your whereabouts could not be tracked and that pressing matters of credit needed to be resolved."

Emma shifted daintily in her chair, taking only a few moments to let the news that James had relayed to her sink in.

"Then we will go to this law firm and resolve this at once," she said standing. "And you will accompany me, Mr. Knox, at which time we will reassign ownership of *Lavender Blue* to myself."

James Knox wiped beads of sweat from his brow.

"Yes, and we should do so with utmost haste," he replied.

"Please bill this to the *Lavender Blue* estate," he told the waiter, who removed the bill from their table and nodded in silent agreement.

CHAPTER EIGHT

HOME

With a minimum of delay, facilitated by Hershell Brownston's detailed will and testament, by day's end the deed to *Lavender Blue* was fully assigned to Emma Brownston, who then took advantage of the convenience of her visit to the estate's law firm to formally transfer overseer duties to her trusted servant, James Knox.

For a moment as she sat in the law office, a vision of a herself and Hershell as newlyweds running hand in hand through the lavender fields flashed through her mind, but she quickly dismissed it. The two had married after the briefest of courtships with her smitten by the attentions of a gentleman clearly established in life and he by the youthful exuberance she brought to his world.

She wasn't sure when he had grown bored with her, but for years they had lived separate lives to avoid the scandal of divorce until he had forced her hand on that one night of abandoned restraint that had prompted her to finally leave—not so much out of fear as out of the need to spend what remained of her life free of the prison his dalliance and indifference had created.

She returned her attention to James Knox as they stood, thanked the attorney, and departed. After a quick lunch, they took the next train to Sutton and from there traveled by horse-drawn coach to the estate, in reverse of the way she had left in the spring.

Emma smelled the lavender before she saw the fields, a prelude to the conflicted joy she felt at being home. She had always loved the farm. Once, before they were married and while they still retained the passion of youth, Hershell had promised it to her and to her surprise, he had kept his word. The irony of it now being fully hers despite the deterioration of their relationship was not lost as the buggy bounced along the dusty road to the main gate.

Now *Lavender Blue* was really hers—fully, totally, and indisputably. Had that been enough to resolve her contempt for the man she had once pledged to love forever, it would have been grand, but underlying the joy of her return was the lingering remembrance of her husband's boots on the servant Colleen's stoop and his own dismissive words as he had left her crying in their bed in the weeks before she had fled the estate.

She watched James as he opened the gate, took the carriage through, and then disembarked to close it again. His movements were deft and marked with the ease of one who had set the roots of comfort into his surroundings. She watched him grab the reins and gently prod the horses into a slow trot. Ahead she saw Miriam running to greet him with both children running beside her as they called out to their father and the oldest one grabbed the reins to help guide the horses to a stop. My, but the boys had grown since Emma had last seen them!

At that moment she knew she had done right by James in appointing him overseer, just as she knew that he would do right by her in the same way that he had always kept a respectful watch over her well-being.

"Daddy! Daddy!" she heard the youngest child call.

In one fell swoop, James embraced them all—Miriam and each of his sons, before bringing them to the coach, helping her down, and reintroducing Emma to his family.

She stopped Miriam mid-curtsey and told her in the gentlest way that the wife of the overseer curtsied to no one but the queen. She tousled the blond curls of the younger child, who pulled away as if he were too old for such attention.

When the group had made their way to the cabin occupied by the family, Emma offered the appropriate compliments about its cleanliness and homespun appeal, then in a move that surprised even her, told them that such a small cottage was not grand enough for the overseer of *Lavender*

Blue and instructed James to immediately begin the selection of whatever parcel of land he loved most, upon which he should immediately begin the construction of a fitting home at the expense of the estate and to waste no time so that it could be finished before winter.

Because her arrival had been unexpected, the main house was closed up and musty, but Miriam quickly went to work, summoning additional help from the servants to throw open the windows, dust the furniture, and prepare fresh linens for the bed.

By nightfall, Emma Brownston was home and ready to begin the next phase of her life in a way that would not have seemed possible only six months ago. As nighttime's quiet prevailed, she snuffed out the flame in her oil lamp and climbed between the freshly laundered sheets of the bed.

As familiar as was the pungent smell of the oil lamp, modern trends dictated that its use was rapidly becoming outdated. Perhaps she would discuss the possibility of bringing electricity to the farm with James one day soon—that and a few other ideas that would bring the farm to its optimal status in the dawning industrial age of the early twentieth century.

CHAPTER NINE

HOLDER OF THE DEED

No one in Skagway had heard from Emma Brownston in the weeks since she had left, even though two sternwheelers had already come and gone on the river. So by late August, when the men of Skagway were firming up plans for their hunting trip and the women were working feverishly to smoke or dry the salmon, most thoughts of Emma Brownston had vanished.

In high places, the berries had been ripe for weeks and afternoons that had a month earlier been spent by women taking their children into the hills for an afternoon of berry picking were now filled with gatherings in kitchens across the area where steaming pots of cranberries, salmonberries, blueberries, and crowberries filled the air with the sweet aromas of fall.

Hans Derrkstad might have succeeded in his efforts to stop thinking about Emma if young Lars would have let him, but when Hans tried to help him with his letters and numbers in preparation for his entering first grade, Lars would simply lower his head and say, "I need Miss Emma to help me remember."

No amount of coaxing from Hans or from anyone in the village could get young Lars to study like he had when Emma Brownston had been there. One day, out of sheer desperation, Hans had punished the boy with three quick whacks with a switch to the backside, which the boy withstood with such stoic resistance that it sent Hans Derrkstand into a weeks-long period of remorse.

"Spare the rod and spoil the child," one older woman advised on learning of the incident, but Hans had never been one to embrace corporal punishment and although it soon became apparent that his son knew this and sometimes took advantage of that knowledge, he took control of his own emotions and vowed to never paddle Lars again.

"I'll reason with you until your head bursts—or mine," he had then told his son, "but on our family's bible I swear I will never take a paddle to you again."

After that young Lars began to apply himself to his learning, which pleased Hans even as he worried whether his son could ever fully trust him again.

Then one day, with Lars now in school and the mercantile busy with fall sales, the fifth sternwheeler of the summer arrived, bringing with it a letter from Britain addressed to the townspeople of Skagway in the name of Hans Derrkstad.

Dear Mr. Derrkstad, Yun and Chan Yang, and Skagway friends,
An emergency situation has brought me back to Britain and although I left abruptly, giving you no explanation, it is my fervent hope that each of you will indulge me with your forgiveness and know that I am safe.
Sincerely,
Emma Brownston

"The letter, it say nothing," Chan Yang fumed. "Who she think she fooling?"

Hans Derrkstad understood Chan Yang's frustration. He felt the same way. The letter said nothing, serving to do no more than to ask for forgiveness for something vague, so no one knew what to forgive.

He read it again. It had been written on a high-grade parchment that was almost never found in the Alaska Territory, and the embossed top revealed that it had been sent from:

Lavender Blue
Hershell Brownston, Proprietor
9 Route 3
South Sutton, England

Hans Derrkstad studied the letterhead. Who was Hershell Brownston? Was he the father or brother to Emma? No, that could not be, for she had clearly said that she was widowed, which would make the proprietor of *Lavender Blue* some relation to her dead husband. Perhaps she had gone to settle her husband's affairs. Why had he not thought of that already?

On some level his heart lightened and his shoulders lifted at the thought. For the first time in weeks, a smile parted his lips. Emma would return, he told himself, and the thought made his heart soar with a most unexpected rush of hope.

For reasons he could not explain, he withdrew from the hunting trip the next day, telling the others that he couldn't risk leaving his son behind should some ill fate intervene. He would, he told them, lend his full support with the processing of game and the cleaning and repairing of equipment that would surely be necessary when everyone returned, but he would remain behind wishing godspeed to all.

When Emma hadn't returned by the time the hunting party left, he called himself a fool, and when nary a word from her presented by their return, he actively began removing all thoughts of the mysterious British woman from his consciousness, even opening his heart to the possibility that surely there were many eligible women in Skagway who would make not only a fine wife, but a wonderful and loving mother to Lars.

Chapter Ten

May Auld Acquaintance . . .

As the raucous sound of New Year's celebrations rang through camp No. 1 and reverberated up and down every street in the now booming town of Skagway, Alaska, Hans Derrkstad sat in his office going over the books for the mercantile.

Although electricity was now available in the center of town, he preferred to work by the light of one of the seal oil candles that he had acquired on a recent trip to Nome, and so as the numbers flickered on the pages of the ledger before him, he let his mind drift to thoughts of days past.

Julia, his wife, had been his first and only love. They had married when she was only sixteen and her loss at the tender age of twenty-nine had left him older than his own thirty-two years and devoid of much hope for the future. If not for his love of the young son Julia had named Lars even before his birth, Hans Derrkstad might have faded into the gray oblivion of loneliness that so regularly threatened to overpower his soul.

Young Lars was growing up quickly and would be turning six this year of 1912, and Hans would be turning thirty-eight a short week later. From his perspective, he might as well have been facing extinction, as he had let his appearance suffer, his clothing fall into disrepair, and the hair on his face grow unchecked, its color of emerging gray doing little to add to his overall persona.

He heard something rumble lightly in the next room and lifted the metal holder with its seal oil candle from his desk before walking into the workroom beside his office. Out of the corner of his eye, he saw a mouse scurry by—a vole, actually, the sub-Arctic's version of mice.

He pulled the curtain back slightly to see that the winter storm was still raging, and then nodded his head in acceptance of the rodent's need to seek shelter from the cold. On the way back to his office, he brushed past a basket of sealskins that his skin sewers would soon be fashioning into parkas, and then past the industrial sewing machine that had been left mostly unused since Emma'a departure.

He swallowed the lump that was forming in his throat at the thought of her. Why could he not get her out of his mind? He had known her for such a short time before her departure and for her brief stay in Skagway she had been mostly troubled as well as reclusive—the complete opposite of Julia with her lighthearted exuberance for life. He choked back tears at the memory of his beloved wife and shifted his thoughts back to Emma.

She had shown every sign of emerging from the shadow under which she had arrived, and hadn't the old church ladies even embraced her in a way he had seldom seen before, seemingly because of her lilting voice and her rumored association as a couturier for the Queen of England? Certainly she was more beautiful and more interesting than most of the women who lived in Skagway, and more attentive in her deference to him than any of the others had been in their pursuit of a wealthy widower.

He set the candleholder back down on his desk and quickly scanned his books, making a few notations before reaching for his stationery and his favorite quill tip pen.

Over the next hour, slowly and methodically, he filled one page and then another of the birch parchment paper using black ink from the well on his desk. When he was done, he sealed his words with parchment paper and a roller, waited until he was certain it was dry, and folded the document inside a matching envelope, which he then sealed with wax.

He sat there for what seemed like an interminable amount of time before he pinched out the flame twice for good measure and pulled his jacket off the peg by the door. By the time he had put on his wool cap and wrapped a long woolen scarf around his face and neck, the church bells were ringing in the New Year.

Quickly he turned the key in the lock of the shop door and scurried home, determined to get there before the crowd spilled into the streets.

After a quick check on the sleeping Lars, he stoked the fire, turned his own bed down, climbed inside, donned a nightcap, and let the heavy fur comforter cover him from toe tips to chin. Then he drank the poison he had mixed into a warm and comforting drink that afternoon, hoping that Chan Yang and her husband would find the letter he had tucked under their door before the fire that warmed his son went out the next day and before the boy could find him—all this as he prayed they would understand his need to be with Julia again.

CHAPTER ELEVEN

THE BOY

With most of the town of Skagway asleep after a long night of welcoming in the new year, few if any saw Chan Yang scurry with a blanket-wrapped Lars from Hans Derrkstad's home to her own in the early hours of the first day of 1912. With the mercantile suddenly shuttered closed, it only took a day or so before most everyone in town had heard that Hans Derrkstad had been found dead in his bed and that the young boy, Lars, would be staying indefinitely with the Yangs.

Although the whispers of "So sad," "Poor boy," and the lot were often heard around Skagway, no one intervened or questioned the Yangs' relationship with the young Lars once Chan Yang declared after Hans Derrkstad's funeral, "He leave the boy with me."

An autopsy later would show that Hans Derrkstad had died of acute hemlock poisoning and that he had also fallen victim to consumption, which on examination, had proven to be extensive.

Although the women of the Methodist-Episcopal church made a concerted effort to make sure that Lars attended school and that the Yangs had adequate help with clothing and feeding him, after a month or two the young boy was no longer seen in school, but was instead working in the Yang Laundry most days and evenings.

Every once in a while, though, during quiet parts of the day, people would report hearing Lars Derrkstad singing quietly as he worked:

One plus two
Plus three plus four
Makes for ten
Let's count some more . . .

And every so often, someone would slip a textbook under the back door of the laundry in hopes that the young boy would be able to absorb new knowledge.

As the Yangs were honorable people, Emma Brownston's apartment, having been secured with a rental payment for one full year by Hans Derrkstad, remained empty—causing regular speculation as to whether or not Emma Brownston planned to return.

Chan Yang, for her part, remained tight-lipped about the whole situation, simply repeating the same information whenever asked, "Woman not who she say she was," before shaking her head in dismay.

Although final disposition of the business had not yet been determined, after a month the mercantile reopened, with the skin sewers that Hans Derrkstad had hired taking on a more prominent role in operations, while an accountant maintained the books under the oversight of Hans Derrkstad's attorney.

Before long, the remaining stock of Brownston bags had sold out and had been replaced with kuspuks, seal skin mittens, vests, and hats, and assorted items of beaded jewelry.

Come early February, Chan Yang began openly expressing her frustration at being responsible for the child and there were rumors that the young Lars had run away on at least two occasions, causing a great deal of consternation for the Yangs and whispers that they would soon be seeking an orphanage in which to place the boy.

Lars was six now and given to expressing himself in new ways. He liked to call out to some of the miners after watching them drop off their laundry, sometimes begging for gold in exchange for some small job—like folding their clothes, or running to get them when they were done.

A couple of the older women in town, after conferring with Chan Yang, had begun bringing books by and spending time helping Lars with his reading skills. Although this usually went pretty well, on more than one occasion, Lars had stolen money from their purses—an accusation vehemently denied by Chan Yang, that is, until she stumbled on a stash of gold coins in the boy's room one day and was forced to admit that the ladies' claims about the young boy's delinquency were, in fact, true.

By mid-February, after one especially harrowing incident with Lars, Chan Yang had reached the peak of her frustration and had mailed off a letter to England.

Chapter Twelve
The Letter

The letter from Skagway arrived at *Lavender Blue Estates* on April 2, 1912. Emma readily recognized the return address as being that of Chan and Yun Yang's residence, but she was unable to read the letter that was written in Chinese. Perhaps someone in London would be able to help.

The paper and the envelope in which the letter arrived had been sealed with wax and bore the customary postmarks of international travel. Although the paper was somewhat crumpled around the edges, it had arrived in excellent condition considering the route it had traveled by steamship, stage, and train.

Emma tucked the letter into the top drawer of her bureau before noticing that not all the pages were the same. Slowly she unfolded it again only to find that two pages were written in English with a meticulous and articulate hand. She shuffled the two to see the signature, surprised to learn it was that of Hans Derrkstad.

She wondered how he was, if he had received her letter, and smiled at the thought of the young Lars. Surely the boy would have mastered his numbers by now and be well on his way to acquiring excellent reading skills. Wouldn't he be about six now? First grade!

Emma looked at Chan Yang's letter again, but instead of placing it back in the bureau, she folded it and laid it on the table by the door. Why had Chan Yang written and why had she included a letter from

Hans Derrkstad? She had sent her address, and he could have written her himself if he chose. Perhaps he was angry at the fact that she had left.

She looked at his letter again. It was addressed to no one. It was simply there, with thoughts poured out onto paper in the meticulous handwritten script of one who was known for being fastidious and well controlled.

Tomorrow she would take Chan Yang's letter to London and look for an interpreter, but for right now, she might as well read the one from Hans Derrkstad. She stood to summon her housemaid, but decided she could boil her own water for tea. While the water was boiling, she cut up a lemon and took down some sugar from the shelf. She had never cared for milk in her tea the way Hershell had. Funny that something as simple as making tea made her remember him.

She placed the teapot, a cup, and a spoon on a serving tray and carried them to her sitting room, where she sat in the wooden rocker with tapestry-padded seat, armrests, and back that had been her mother's. Then she put her feet up on the small matching stool, poured herself a cup of the brew, and began to read.

On this auspicious occasion of the closing of the year of 1911 as I stand on the threshold of 1912, my thoughts are heavy as another year passes without my dear Julia, loving wif,e and mother to our son, Lars.

Oh, had she been here for these past six years to see our son grow and for me to selfishly feel her love. Surely, she would have balanced me with her gentility as she always did, and perhaps spared me from having taken a strap to the boy. Although I know I used utmost restraint, I see the hurt in his young eyes and will always regret the lifting of my hand to him.

The mercantile . . .

Emma skimmed over the several paragraphs that described the financial status of the mercantile, pages intended for the eyes of an accountant or— no! Not a survivor!

She hurried ahead along the page, but there was more about the shop, so she stood up, walked to the window and back, went to the kitchen to freshen her tea, sitting down slightly less comfortably into the rocker when she returned.

She reread the first part of the letter and felt tears come to her eyes. Hans Derrkstad had known true love and without it—well, did she even need to read further? She rocked back and forth for several minutes, summoned her own courage, and read on.

I had so hoped to find love again and surely the arrival of Miss Emma had given me hope that I might find love for both me and my son, but I have seen that hope vanish, and although I have secured her apartment for the next one year, I fear that she did not herself feel the spark I thought was there and has fled to an old life, or a new life, or some life other than here.

By now Emma was fully engulfed in sorrow. Without knowing how this letter would end, she knew. She wiped her eyes and continued reading.

And so to Chan Yang and Yun Yang I entrust the care of my Lars as I direct them to a sizeable sum held secure at The First Bank of Skagway. I plead with them to raise my boy with integrity and honor and to continue the fine education begun by Miss Emma in the back of my own mercantile.

Please know that I have loved my life as I have loved my son, but that without my wife and my son's mother, I choose not to go on. Always tell him his father was weak, not strong, but that he was weak in being overburdened with a love that he could no longer carry in this mortal life.

Instructions for my remains will be found on the backside of this document. With sound mind and heartfelt appreciation for God's life until now, Hans Petr Derrkstad, Esq.

CHAPTER THIRTEEN

INTERPRETING CHINESE

Emma made the hours-long trip into London in a carriage driven by *Lavender Blue* overseer, James Knox. The trip was filled mostly with small talk as details of estate business queries for their attorney had already been hammered out.

James had completed the home for Miriam and his family before winter and remarked as they drove along at how grateful the family was to have received such consideration from the estate, this not being the first time he had expressed such appreciation.

Emma's home had received few updates other than the removal of all traces of Hershell's influence and the demolition of the servant's cottage, which had stood as a constant reminder of his infidelities. Although nearly a century old, the main house she occupied was well constructed, comfortable, and roomy, and Emma relished her time there behind the mature formal gardens that had stood for longer than she had been on this earth.

The new servants' quarters were far different from the earlier row of individual cottages that had stood at *Lavender Blue* for nearly a hundred years. It had been James who had suggested a large estate-style building with individual apartments built around a huge common area. Not only did this common area contain flower and vegetable gardens, it had a central play area for the children, whose squeals were buffered by the surrounding vegetation, which also allowed their parents to supervise them as they worked in the gardens. Each apartment also had a private balcony that overlooked the lavender fields and the winding Thames River off in the distance.

The new design also made it much easier to install modern amenities, such as electricity, running water, and central heating. Although the old cabins had been the best for their day, they were beginning to fall into disrepair, and so for both esthetic and personal reasons, Emma had approved their demolition and embraced James's new design.

The servants at *Lavender Blue* had long enjoyed deluxe accommodations and had never failed to repay the generosity of the proprietors with loyalty and diligence. Surrounded by acres and acres of sweet-smelling lavender fields, a position at *Lavender Blue Estates* was a coveted position indeed.

Emma fingered Chan Yang's letter in her pocket with every hope she would find an interpreter in London. When she failed to do so after two long days, she decided to approach the Chinese Embassy and ask for their assistance.

Unfortunately, that assistance would require more effort than she had imagined as she learned the difficult truth that Chinese was one of the hardest languages to interpret—a reality marked by variations in descriptive words, regional dialects, and its very obscure use in the modern world.

At best, she learned, the letter could be forwarded to a linguistics expert at Oxford, who would undoubtedly opt to send it or a copy of it to Chinese experts at one of the universities there—a process that could take weeks, if not months.

Emma furrowed her brow as she thought of Hans Derrkstad, his note, and the letter from Chan Yang.

"I don't mean to be either impudent or intrusive, but is something troubling you, Mrs. Brownston?" James finally asked. "You have seemed exceedingly distracted during our long trip together. I do hope that is not a reflection of your satisfaction with my services, because should I be underperforming in any area, then . . ."

Emma placed one hand gently on James's forearm, embarrassed that she had failed to disguise her troubled soul.

"Oh, dear James," she began. "The fact that you are here managing all aspects of *Lavender Blue Estates*, and doing so with such finesse and diligence is more a blessing to me than perhaps I deserve."

James loosened his jaw and relaxed his shoulders. What, then, could be troubling the woman who now owned the estate to which he had pledged his eternal loyalty?

"Thank you, ma'am . . ."

"Please, James, unless we are involved in public discussion directly related to your representation of the farm, please just call me Emma."

"Yes, ma'am, er, Emma."

James stumbled across the words, lacking the temerity to openly dismiss his years of subservience to both the estate and to Hershell Brownston himself.

"The fact of the matter is that I received some disturbing news in last week's mail and now find myself in the position of wondering just what I should feel about what I have learned," Emma said, laughing nervously.

"I'm sure you're even more confused now than ever, Mr. Knox."

James cast a look her way before coaxing the horses into a trot. He enjoyed driving the carriage and took the next three curves on the trail at a faster speed than he normally might have before pulling the reins back and slowing down.

"It's not my place to impose," he stated.

"You're a wonderful man, James Knox, and you have a wonderful young family. I could not be more proud to have you as overseer of our beloved *Lavender Blue*." James smiled and nodded, keeping both hands on the reins.

"At some point I may decide to tell you more about what I am thinking," Emma Brownston said, "but first I must figure out exactly what that is for myself."

Chapter Fourteen

Alaska Bound

By the time Emma and James were turning down the winding dirt road to *Lavender Blue*, Emma had made up her mind.

"I know I haven't talked much about why I went to Alaska," she began, "and it seems unnecessary to share many of those details with you now."

James shifted in his seat and pulled back a little on the reins, causing the carriage to slow to a crawl. Although no one had ever mentioned or dared to discuss the infidelities of Hershell Brownston, it was no secret to anyone at *Lavender Blue* that he had fathered a child with the servant, Colleen. This matter had required his direct knowledge, as it was he who as overseer had made the final settlement offer with Colleen on behalf of the estate.

"But without going into too much detail, and because you are, after all, the overseer of *Lavender Blue*, I want you to know that I have decided to leave on the next steamship to Alaska in about fourteen days," Emma said.

"I see," James nodded. "And will your absence be lengthy?"

"This I cannot predict," Emma answered, "and I have no intention of making my absence permanent. However, I have unsettled matters in Skagway that I would like to reconcile in full while I am there." This time James nodded but did not speak.

"It will surely be for the duration of the summer," Emma continued, "but beyond that, I really am not able to predict if any and what circumstances might serve to keep me there longer."

"I understand," James again replied.

"I'll make sure that you have everything you need to manage the estate as well as provisional control until I return, subject to the final authority of our attorney, of course. It's important for you to know that I trust you implicitly, James, but that for your own protection and for mine, we will have a formal plan."

"And what should I tell the staff?" James asked.

"That I am about on personal business and recreation will suffice," Emma answered.

"Yes, ma'am," James nodded.

The fact that she had divulged even a smidgeon of her personal plans disturbed Emma, for although there was no more trustworthy person on this earth, her inclination to secretiveness had become even more deeply entrenched over the past year.

Perhaps this was exacerbated by the fact that she was not even sure herself why she was determined to return to Alaska except for acknowledging the old adage, *once you visit Alaska you will always return.*

CHAPTER FIFTEEN
NO SUFFRAGETTE

Emma's arrival in New York was as exciting as she had hoped and she spent several days there visiting first-class shops and restaurants, including one very interesting store that specialized in outdoor and survival gear for women.

During her past visit to Skagway, she had found it necessary to rely on men's stores to outfit herself with durable boots, pants, and outerwear, but this shop was unique in that it offered outdoor wear it advertised as *for the modern, pioneer woman.*

There she purchased several pairs of oiled canvas pants and one long skirt made of similar waterproof and windproof material, as well as a matching jacket, wide-brimmed felt hat, and two pairs of sturdy leather boots. If she had ever been unsure about how long her visit to Alaska would be, her purchases signaled it would be for much longer than one or two weeks.

She had just left the store when two women, themselves dressed in rather plain clothing for New York, pushed her into an alley under the guise of discussing what one of them described as "your obvious situation as a fleeing suffragette."

"We're here to help," one of them warned. "The police are everywhere, looking out for thin, frail women like you. They'll try to rescue you from the ravages of your hunger strikes."

"The rest of us? Hunger strikes?" Emma asked.

"We suffragettes. Our movement has just now reached the shores of the United States from Britain. We're growing by the day and we sometimes use hunger strikes to make our point."

Emma was taken aback. Due to the remoteness of *Lavender Blue Estates*, she had largely avoided the burgeoning suffragette movement in Britain and although secretly happy at the hard-fought battle to win women the vote, she harbored no desire to push the limits of that privilege into the arena of political activism.

She coughed, as was often the case when she was under stress.

"They've force-fed you already, haven't they? Arletta, she's one of us," one of the women said, calling to a friend who had scurried down the alley as if fleeing from some unknown threat.

"You'll be safe with us," the woman assured Emma.

Emma smiled faintly as she continued to walk slowly away from the clutch of women, watching as the one they called Arletta lifted a sign from behind some trashcans and headed her way. Emma caught a glimpse of the sign: *No Vote, No Food!*

Emma knew her frailness had come from her long battle with consumption—an affliction that showed all signs of having cured itself, although it had left her pale and thin—and not from a hunger strike, but she declined to explain, saying nothing.

She listened politely as the two women who had cornered her ranted on about women's rights and the evil suppression they would no longer endure, before finding her escape when a nattily dressed man walked by. She smiled at the stranger as she stepped out from the alley, and looped her arm through his.

"Darryl, darling," she said. "I feared you had taken a wrong turn."

Before the man could recover from his surprise, she had unhooked her arm from his and ducked into a nearby department store, where she lost herself in the women's lingerie department before finally leaving a few hours later.

What was becoming of this world anymore? By the time she boarded the Transcontinental Railroad passenger car for the trip west, she had procured a derringer for her bag with plans to pick up something even more substantial once she reached her destination. For now the pearl-handled muff gun would have to suffice, but at least it was some protection against those in society who wished to prey on a woman alone.

And so as she set forth on the *SS Princess Sophia* on the 19th of May, 1912 Emma Brownston by way of her long journey, had taken the first steps towards independence, suffragette movement or not.

This time she had come better prepared, traveling with two steamer trunks instead of one simple bag, and carrying a satchel full of American dollars that she had accepted in exchange for her British pounds.

Somehow she had bypassed any real trouble during her travels and was now safely onboard the steamship bound for the District of Alaska, where such matters as women's rights and voting were likely irrelevant to the hordes of fortune seekers focused on survival and the acquisition of riches from the gold fields so prevalent there.

Chapter Sixteen

Sailin', Sailin'

The first day of the trip was uneventful with Emma spending much of her time catching up on her reading, but by the second day, thoughts of what she might face in Skagway began to surface. That night, unable to sleep, she donned a long down coat over her sleeping gown and stepped outside her stateroom to look at the stars.

The air was cold and brisk as if foretelling a coming snowfall. She took notice of the clear skies and knew that the stars held a different forecast. Fortunately, the wind was calm, so she ventured several feet down the outer deck before hearing footsteps and ducking into an alcove where the lifeboats were stored.

"*Sailing, sailing, over the ocean blue* . . ." a man's voice sang loudly with the bawdy exuberance that alcohol often brings.

"You wouldn't be singin' like that if ya hadn't stole my poke, Smitty."

"Aw, c'mon, Jake, it weren't stealin' less'n I didn't spend the half of it buyin' yer shots tonight, now, an' ya know it. *Sailin' sailin'* . . . c'mon, man, . . . *over the ocean* . . ."

"Stealin's stealin', Smitty, and no thievin' drunk's gonna tell me different, ya hear?"

A loud pop pierced the air, followed by a second pop, a moan, and the sound of a thud hitting the deck. Emma froze in place, terrified and afraid to even breathe. She heard the sound of running steps, more sounds of a struggle, and then quiet. When she peeked around the corner, she saw two uniformed men with lanterns scanning the deck, while two others were hauling a body in the opposite direction, and yet two more were leading away a man with his hands tied behind his back.

She ducked back into the alcove and began to shiver, letting out an uncontrollable sigh in the process. She saw the light from the lanterns bouncing off the deck as their glow pierced the shadows and she cringed as the sound of footsteps drew near. She shrank back even more as the light from one of the lanterns stopped short of exposing her position. Her relief was short-lived, for a moment later the light flashed past her again, this time illuminating the full length of her figure in the shadows.

Just then the ship's horn blew and she screamed.

"Hey, Joe, bring me a blanket, would ya," one of the men bearing lanterns called.

Someone appeared with a blanket, which one of the men helped wrap around Emma.

"You're safe, ma'am. We're the ship's security. What you saw you shoulda never had to see, but every once in a while it happens when a couple of blue tickets, who somehow never got off in Seattle, decide to deal their version of frontier justice on board. Trying to get back to Alaska by hook or by crook, ya know."

Emma looked puzzled.

"The District of Alaska is set to become a territory this year and scofflaws and gold thieves are no longer welcome there and they're giving them blue tickets—one-way tickets out.

"Alaska, ma'am, is on its way to having representation in the Congress of these United States. It *is* a moment in history."

Prior to this, Emma had given little thought to the politics or governmental status of Alaska. For her, it had been a place of wilderness solitude and had served as her personal retreat from the centuries-old aristocracy into which she had been born.

Driven to this extreme by personal circumstances and her seemingly insurmountable health crises, she had fled to Skagway for no other reason than to experience for herself the pioneering adventure of the gold rush before she would no longer be well enough to travel.

There, too, she could be free from Hershell's control even as she knew that he would find her no matter to what reaches of the earth she might roam.

All of that was history now with her husband's death, and even her own brief stay in Skagway remained more a memory than a reality with the passing of Hans Derrkstad and the distancing of Chan and Yun Yang from her life.

Perhaps this visit would serve as a type of closure. Perhaps she would arrive in Skagway and remember why she had come there in the first place. Or perhaps, the call of the wild had infected her soul, just as it had so many others before her.

"I thank you for the blanket and the consideration, sir," she told the security officer at the door to her stateroom. "May I keep it for warmth for now and return it in the morning?"

The guard nodded as he assisted her through the door, waiting only a brief moment to hear her latch the lock before walking away. Emma listened to his fading footsteps as she pulled the blanket tightly around her and fell into a deep, if not fitful sleep.

CHAPTER SEVENTEEN

SURPRISE

When the *Sophia* reached Skagway, early signs of summer were just beginning to appear. Although the shallow lakes still had a layer of slop ice covering all but their edges, the trees held fat buds ready to explode in leafy splendor as soon as there was no more threat of frost. The days were now longer, too, with the extra light another way for nature to declare that winter was indeed gone.

Emma hiked her skirt to keep it from dragging in the mudholes that pitted the street. At least she had changed into her new boots after having hesitated about pairing them with the delicate fabric of her skirt. How quickly she had forgotten how dirty Alaska could be and how quickly had that reality been brought back to her since her arrival.

She had left her two trunks in secure storage at the dock. No sense lugging them around until she knew where she was going to stay. A horse-drawn buggy clipped by, swerving only slightly in an effort to avoid her, and splashing mud up onto her skirt. Thank goodness for the Yang laundry, which was located next door to where she was heading right now.

Although a few people nodded as she walked by, no one seemed to recognize her—a reality she found somewhat disconcerting. She had been gone less than a year, but even she had to admit that her time in Skagway had been short and monumental to no one but herself.

She heard another carriage approaching and hiked her skirt up again.

"Ma'am," a male voice said as the carriage passed by.

Quickly, she moved toward the boardwalk that had suddenly emerged in front of a string of businesses along the road.

"May I assist, ma'am?" A stoop-shouldered man with a scraggly beard, called from the closest storefront.

Emma avoided his outstretched hand as she climbed the two wooden stairs to the boardwalk. She then nodded slightly, before straightening her skirt and moving down the walkway towards town.

She heard a cough, then the ping of a spittoon and resisted the urge to glare at whoever had chosen to engage in the act of spitting in her presence, and then only out of deference to the possible plight of the perpetrator, who she hypothesized, might well be in the same situation with consumption as she had found herself in just one year ago. Then she straightened her shoulders, sharpened her resolve, and continued toward the residence of Chan and Yun Yang.

Her pace slowed when she saw it. It was much as she remembered it, only slightly more weathered by the harsh winter and still surrounded by mounds of dirty crystallized snow that had splotches of greening grass sprouting from the edges.

Emma climbed the three wooden stairs to the front porch, stepping carefully onto each of the weathered boards pockmarked by the heads of nails that local men pounded into the soles of their boots to keep from slipping on the frosty surface. She straightened her skirt, adjusted her hat, and rapped lightly on the door.

There was no answer, so she knocked again, this time harder. Still there was no answer. She moved sideways and peered into the window. The living room was shadowy, blocked from any sunlight by large boards that had been nailed across the deck end to block wind and blowing snow in the winter.

Only the sight of two teacups on a table in the dining area just past the living room gave any evidence that someone had recently been there.

She went back to the door and knocked again. Still there was no answer.

Just as she was turning around to leave, she heard a commotion around the side of the house.

"What you want? No solicitors!"

Emma saw Chan Yang hurry around the corner of the house. She was without a coat and was wiping her hands with a dishtowel, which she tucked into the pocket of her apron a moment later.

"I too busy to come here. Everyone know I'm at shop all day. What you want?"

By now Emma was walking toward the woman.

"It's me, Emma," she said.

Chan Yang stopped, as if to absorb the impact of what she saw.

"Emma," she said softly, before engaging in a barrage of words that left Emma no time to respond.

"You get my letter? You not answer? No courtesy to answer? Sent months ago. First you leave, then you not respond. I don't know. Not who you say. That's what I tell Yun Yang, woman not who she say."

Emma lowered her head and let Chan Yang exhaust her spiel. When she finally spoke, it was softly and with an air of contriteness in her voice.

She told Chan Yang that she had received her letter and apologized for leaving so suddenly and without explanation. She offered to pay for any outstanding expenses that had been incurred on her behalf and then suggested that she and Chan Yang might go somewhere indoors to talk.

"Sure. Okay. Room paid for by Mr. Derrkstad for one year. Still have three months and one week," Chan Yang said in her most businesslike tone.

Emma followed as Chan Yang walked to her apartment, inserted a key, opened the door, and led them inside.

"I air out once a month, but it still stale," she said, cracking a couple of windows and running her dishtowel over some of the furniture as they passed by.

"Go ahead, sit," she said to Emma. "I make tea."

Chapter Eighteen

"You Not Who You Say"

While the water boiled, Chan Yang ran next door to tell her husband what was keeping her so long. Emma mulled over their most recent encounter, trying to imagine how she would feel if someone had deceived her the way she had deceived the people of Skagway.

But what did any of that really matter? Wasn't it a well-known fact that those who chose to live in the far reaches of the northern hemisphere were either wildly adventurous or for some reason had chosen to remove themselves from mainstream society? Did frontier life ensure survival of the fittest, or did it simply assure survival of the strongest?

Where else but in a place like this could the seemingly impossible happen—like the many stories she had heard of former streetwalkers rising up from the dark and bawdy life on the streets to a permanent status as the wife of the local banker, doctor, lawyer, and so forth?

Had she, in her fervor to escape the wiles of her cheating husband and the unwanted pregnancy he had forced upon her really been deceitful, or had she fled due to some inherent sense that she could survive only if she could find a life as far removed as possible from the constraints of the one she had left?

The sounds of Chan Yang's return jolted her away from her reflections.

"Chan Yang, I would like to talk to you about my time here—and about your letter."

"Brought broom. So much dust," Chan Yang spouted.

"I was hoping . . ."

"No time, Miss Emma. Chan Yang care less. Business to run."

Emma sipped her tea. Chan Yang had always shown a tendency to subvert emotion and to see life in black and white terms only, and this time was no exception.

"Can you at least tell me about Mr. Derrkstad, and Lars?"

"Wrote in letter. All I know," she answered, continuing to straighten the apartment.

"You stay until rent due in three months' time, then you find new place."

Chan Yang paused and looked Emma directly in the eye as if to emphasize her point.

"Okay," Emma answered.

"Boy adopted," she said after pausing from her tasks for a moment. "No life for young boy here."

Emma nodded.

"He left one thing for you . . . Mr. Hans."

Emma watched as Chan Yang went into a back room and returned with a small leather case, which she unlatched and from which she removed a key.

"He say to give this to you if you come back," Chan Yang said. "Letter said that. That not why you're here?"

Emma paled and felt a catch in her throat. Did Chan Yang, and perhaps others around town hold such little regard for her integrity that they thought she would come all the way from Britain for someone's last belongings—someone she had only known a short while? Angry at first, she stood and reached for her coat, stopping only to open her purse and hand several gold coins to Chan Yang.

"What this for?" Chan Yang said, looking surprised, before rejecting the coins with a sweep of her hand. "Where you get this? Can't take. Don't want. Can't be bought . . ."

"I want to pay you for your trouble," Emma said, not allowing Chan Yang time to reply. "This is my money. I have lots of money."

Chan Yang stood to leave.

"Chan Yang only take honest money."

Emma felt the welling of tears.

"Chan Yang. You don't understand. You don't know . . ."

"Rent paid by Hans Derrkstad for next three months, then you gone," Chan Yang said with the sweep of her hand. "Mr. Derrkstad gone because of you. Boy gone. Now, time for you."

Emma watched Chan Yang walk out the door before removing her coat and sitting down. She picked up the small leather case left for her by Hans Derrkstad and opened it again. The key was lying on a raised velvet mound. She lifted it and saw a note inside:

To whoever is bequeathed this key, take to Skagway assayer, Rudolph Munson, for further instructions.
Hans Petr Derrkstad, Esq.

Tomorrow she would look for a new place, hopefully one with running water and heat and she would stop to visit Mr. Rudolph Munson at the Assay office, wherever it might be.

CHAPTER NINETEEN

THE KEY

Early the next day, and for the next several days thereafter, Emma roamed the streets of Skagway in search of a new apartment. Despite the fact that the Gold Rush was winding down, Skagway continued to boom.

By the end of the week she had given up all hope of finding something suitable. With the next steamship out not available until August, and having exhausted all options in town, she was left with few choices outside of moving to another community or building herself a cabin.

Her attempts to meet up with Mr. Rudolph Munson had met with no success. On several occasions she had made the long trek to the assay office at the opposite end of town only to find the same note nailed to the door:

CLOSED UNTIL RIVERBOAT REPAIRS COMPLETED. ASSAYER DELAYED IN KLUKWAN.

What was the point of all this? Why had she left a comfortable and secure life in England to come back here? Had it really been to relieve her worry about the boy and his welfare or was there more to it than that?

She knew the answer before the question even cleared her mind, and she knew it as clearly as the up and coming poet Robert Service had when he wrote *Spell of the Yukon*.

THERE'S A LAND—OH, IT BECKONS AND BECKONS,
AND I WANT TO GO BACK—AND I WILL . . .

Of course, there was much more to the poem than that, but right now these were the words that most came to mind. She would have to find in which bag she had stashed the beloved book of poems—that, or buy a new copy sometime soon so she could read on the steamship back to England—or right here in Alaska, whichever came first. Wherever the location of the book, though—as in the poem, Alaska had beckoned her and so she had come back.

The news that young Lars had been adopted had come as a relief. Hopefully he had been taken into a home where he would be loved and educated. The alternative that the boy could just as easily—as she had heard was all too common—have been sold into child labor made her shudder. Would she ever know the truth? A partial answer came from the wife of the skin sewer, who worked alongside her husband in Hans Derrkstad's old mercantile. On one of the many afternoons when Emma stopped by, the skin sewer's wife told her the story.

The boy had lived with the Yangs for almost two months, but on several occasions had run away, once for an entire week. One day after another such episode, a well-dressed man had come and taken the boy away. No one in Skagway had seen either of them since or dared ask the Yangs what had happened out of fear of falling out of favor with the Yangs and losing access to the only laundry services in Skagway.

At first the Yangs had been tight-lipped about the situation, but eventually the story spread that the man had come to adopt the boy and had taken him away from Alaska. Even though curious as to who the people were and where they had taken young Lars, Emma forced thoughts of the boy out of her mind and began to focus solely on her own life. The truth would come out eventually, just as it always had since the beginning of time. Like everyone else, she would have to wait until it did.

It was on a sunny afternoon some two weeks later that she finally saw the door to the assay office open and stepped inside. A tall, slightly stooped man with a serious expression peered at her over his round spectacles as she introduced herself and showed him the key.

"I see," he nodded, coming around the counter to shake her hand. "My name is Rudolph Munson, and Hans Derrkstad, well, he was like a brother to me."

"I was so sorry to hear of his passing," Emma told him, before proceeding to explain the details of why she had previously been in Skagway and why she had left.

"You see, Mr. Munson, I was a woman who was desperately fighting to overcome extreme levels of both fear and betrayal when Mr. Derrkstad took me into his employ. To deny that our relationship was anything beyond professional would be to minimize the feelings I knew he was developing for me. My own situation, being what it was, forced me to maintain utmost restraint in his presence despite my own growing affection for him, lest he should learn that at the time of our meeting I was neither the widow he believed me to be, nor had I arrived under the circumstances that he believed to be true.

"Fate, as it is wont to do, intervened before the situation could escalate when I learned that my own unfaithful husband had died. It was at that time that I fled Skagway, never explaining to a soul and not yet knowing myself if I would ever return.

"The news of Hans's death reached me a few months ago when I saw his letter attached to a letter from Chan Yang that was written in Chinese. For weeks, I looked for someone to interpret the letter for me before deciding to return to Skagway myself, to see exactly what she wanted me to know—that, and with some dedication to ensuring that young Lars would have a suitable home, even if it meant my adopting him myself."

Rudolph Munson rubbed the hair on his meticulously groomed chin and stared at Emma. When he finally spoke, it was with words tinged with measured relief.

"Hans was never able to recover from the loss of his wife, Julia, although he tried valiantly to search for a successor. Eventually, despite his undying love for his son, and not being able to overcome his sense of futility, he sank steadily deeper into the despondence that in his mind removed all hope of future happiness."

"But I never meant to encourage him or give him reason for false assumptions," Emma exclaimed.

"Oh, dear woman, I know that all too well because I knew Hans all too well. No, Miss Emma, you were no more than a refreshing breath of fresh air in this bawdy frontier life. Often Hans would talk of your charming accent, your lilting voice, and your frailty obviously in need of someone to care for you."

"And when I left?"

"When you left, Hans was already struggling with the winter's darkness and some disciplinary issues with the boy that to the average person would have been inconsequential, but to this deeply despondent man, were overwhelming. And so, as the new year rang in, with most townsfolk busy with their revelry, he quietly and methodically stepped over the threshold to join his beloved Julia once more."

"And this key?" Emma asked.

"It belongs to the cabin he built for Julia upriver on the Alaska side of the Canadian border crossing south of Fraser, British Columbia up near the Yukon Territory. It's one hour north by summer train—two in winter. When you are ready, I would like to take you there myself."

Emma nodded before standing, quietly retrieving the key and nodding again before walking out the door into the bright sunlight of late afternoon.

"By the way, Miss Emma," Rudolph Munson called from the doorway, "The boy, Lars, is well. Hans's own cousin, Paul—a doctor—and his barren wife, Anne, adopted him. He will be loved and well cared for and he will receive a proper education. Of this you can be certain."

Chapter Twenty

Arctic White

Emma walked slowly back to Chan Yang's apartment, taking time to wander up and down Skagway's growing number of side streets.

Rudolph Munson bore the qualities of both compassion and integrity. It was as if he epitomized the word *trustworthy*. Already he had eased her mind in revealing that the young Lars was being well cared for.

As far as any issues with the Yangs, well, they believed what they believed and if she were to be honest with herself, she would have to agree she had given those who knew her in Skagway at least some reason to doubt her integrity. In any event, her own life's path had proven she could prevail in the midst of adversity, and although it would be wonderful to regain lost trust, she didn't need it to thrive.

It only took a couple of days for her to decide she would visit the cabin, and so she made arrangements with Rudolph Munson to ride the train with him to the small settlement called *Sven's Crossing* the following Saturday.

The day was bright with the sun's warmth as the train stopped to let them off near a narrow trail that led to an expansive meadow. A smattering of cabins dotted the landscape, the largest of which sat away from the others, overshadowing a smaller cabin surrounded by dog boxes somewhat behind it.

"That's the one," Rudolph Munson said after Emma mentioned the setup. "The big cabin is the one that Hans Derrkstad built for Julia and the small one belongs to a man named Sven Bjorstad and his wife, Daria.

They are longtime friends of Hans, who have cared for this homestead for years. Sven manages a dog team and a small business that operates in the winter to run supplies back and forth to Skagway by train and dogsled."

"Hallo, friend," Sven called as Rudolph helped Emma across a large drainage ditch that ran in front of the property. "Been meanin' to throw some heavy planks across that ditch for some time now."

"Planks'd be nice, my friend," Rudolph Munson said, extending his hand in friendship.

"And ya brought you a lady friend that's prettier than ya deserve," Sven laughed.

"Though pretty she be," Rudolph said, blushing, "she is here on the official business of inspecting the main house that was left to her by our dearly gone Hans Derrkstad."

"God wrap his soul in peace," Sven replied with bowed head.

"My name is Emma Brownston," Emma said, extending her gloved hand.

"Well, my now, but you speak as though from Britain," Sven replied.

"Wembley, to be precise," she answered.

"The fact of the matter is that our friend, Hans, bequeathed this property to Mrs. Brownston, Sven, and so we are here for her to inspect what is rightfully hers and make some decisions on how to best manage this acquisition—if one were to state this in the most neutral of terms."

Sven shifted uncomfortably.

"Please, Mr. Sven, I have no desire to create any level of concern for you or your family. My receipt of the key to this property came as much as a surprise to me as it now appears to be to you," Emma hurried to say.

"I have forgotten my manners," Sven said, "Please come inside my own home, meet my beautiful Daria, and share a cup of tea that she undoubtedly began to brew on seeing you step off the train."

For the next hour or more, Emma sat with Rudolph, Sven, and Daria and learned details about the property that a pending deed would soon list as her own.

She learned that it sat on twelve acres, with the back eight being leased annually to Sven, Daria, and their dogs upon yearly receipt of a certified bank note equal to one troy ounce of pure gold. In keeping with Hans Derrkstad's wishes, the front four acres had been maintained as a homestead, with neat gardens planted around the house and a long a stone walkway to the large ditch, which currently lacked any type of access.

The cabin itself was log and Emma was quick to notice large nails sticking upright from the windowsills and several wooden slats of thick board that had to each be lifted to enter the only door on the side. She also noticed a sign that said, *Arctic White,* above the front door.

"Interesting that there are all those spikes around the windows," she said.

"Not that I'm meanin' to scare you, Mrs. Brownston, but we get our fair share of bears around here most all of spring and fall, and even sometimes in the winter. We all sleep better knowing that once inside our cabins we are mostly safe from them trying to claw their way in."

Emma had heard about bears, but had not yet seen one. Since the spikes looked like a serious deterrent, she had to assume that the bears were somewhat aggressive and also fairly persistent.

"And the sign?"

Sven chuckled.

"Ah, yes, the sign. It seems our friend Hans chose to name his cabin in honor of all the snow we get here in winter," he said. "People around here like to name their cabins. Mine's called *Sven's Crossing*—and folks around here have taken to calling the whole community here by that name. If they're talking about just my cabin, they just say it's *Sven's Crossing* at *Arctic White.*"

Emma nodded and smiled.

"You must be important if the whole community is named after you."

Sven blushed.

"It's more a matter 'a me bein' the only one here most winters and the better part of most springs and falls, too. The rest just come here to hunt, trap or mine—'cept for the doc who comes here just to get away, and who shares his cabin with the railroad bosses from time to time."

The inside of the cabin was more than she had imagined it would be. The walls were log with the chinking in excellent condition thanks to regular maintenance by Sven. Wide-eyed, Emma scanned the large open-beamed interior with its intricately carved posts and benches—including a large bed that even over time sported a comfortable-looking mattress topped with a large, wool-lined fur comforter.

"It has its own well," Sven volunteered, "and an indoor shower and plumbing—a rare pleasure in these parts, but Hans wanted only the best for Julia and so together we built it and made it work."

Although Sven tried to explain the intricacies of the unique plumbing system, those details did not concern Emma except in knowing that it was well designed and far ahead of its day, as well as dependent on neither electricity nor buried tanks.

"It is naturally aerated," Sven proclaimed, "And I am fortunate in having a similar system inside my own cabin."

Emma walked about the room as the men discussed the fine points of the plumbing system. She sat on several of the benches that were strategically placed around the interior, running her hand gently over the hand-carved and smoothly finished surfaces that were equal in their detail to any fine furniture she had seen.

She walked up the hand-hewn stairway to the loft, looking down on the room below and the two men engaged in deep conversation. How was it possible that she had been left not one, but two estates in her inconsequential life—each a full opposite of the other, and each lovingly maintained?

Behind her, the sun poured through a large window that overlooked the entire property, its view enhanced by an enormous spruce tree near the cabin that served to filter the intensity of the sun's rays. She heard the staccato howls of the dogs as she watched Daria dip into a large steaming bucket to put feed into their bowls, smiling as a pet dog tried to help her carry the bucket back to her own cabin.

"Please share your thoughts, Mrs. Brownston," Rudolph Munson called up.

Emma walked down the gently curved stairway built of half-rounds of polished spruce as the men waited for her response.

"I can state with the certainty of a woman's heart that Mrs. Julia Derrkstad was a woman well cared for and that it would be my humble honor to enjoy the luxury of living in this place built on the solid foundation of love."

Sven lowered his head for a moment as if taken aback. No matter the outcome for his own family, this woman belonged here at *Arctic White*.

"He would be pleased to have known your sentiments," Sven Bjorstad said, prompting Emma to reply.

"And it would please me and honor me to know that you would agree to stay on as caretaker and resident, Mr. Bjorstad, but only if you would allow me to pay you a monthly stipend that would include your existing accommodations in return for your services, which at present I see as no different from those you already provide."

Sven Bjorstad removed his hat.

"Are you suggesting that instead of rent you will be paying me?" he said in apparent disbelief.

"That is exactly what I am proposing," Emma replied. "Will you agree?"

"Ma'am," Sven said, "I will not only agree, but I will pledge at this moment on the souls of all who have gone before, to never let you regret the decision to extend this offer to my wife and me."

"Then I will have an agreement to make it official prepared when I return to Skagway," she answered. "And please, please call me Emma . . . you as well, Mr. Munson."

"Yes, ma'am—Emma," both men said simultaneously.

"And will you now call me Rudy?" Rudolph Munson said.

"And Sven for me?" Sven Bjorstad echoed.

"Of course, gentlemen," she replied. "Rudy and Sven."

Chapter Twenty-One

The Train Back

Rudy and Emma reached the tracks just in time to flag down the train to Skagway. Rudy threw their bags on first, and then jumped up onto the platform before reaching down to give Emma a hand up.

"Lucky we ran that last quarter mile," he said as they took their seats. "Otherwise we'd 'a been here all night."

Emma nodded, feeling a wave of fatigue wash over her.

"You'd be wise to invest in a shotgun, a rifle, a revolver, and all its respective ammunition," Rudy said. "And maybe even a horse and a wagon if you can afford it."

When he glanced at Emma, her head was leaned back, her eyes closed, and only the soft inhaling and exhaling of her breath gave any sign of movement.

Rudy laid his own blanket over her. He had never seen a woman so pale that she looked as though she might break in a wind gust or blast of rain. She was thin, too, almost to the point of appearing ill, but the healthy glow in her cheeks and the pinkness in her nail beds said otherwise.

His own wife had died about five years back after contracting typhoid and he had lived alone since, never developing any interest in pursuing romance again. That decision had made his selection as assayer a great job choice, for he had not yet met the woman who would tolerate the constant absence of her husband from their home—necessary absences though they might be.

He laughed inside. Here he was thinking of women when he, at fifty-three, was closer to the grave than he dared even ponder. And she, well he guessed her to be close to forty, but really, he didn't know except that despite her appearance as a mature woman, she had mentioned a pregnancy some while back—and the unfortunate loss of it.

He forced himself to look out the window in an effort to distract himself, admiring the acres and acres of fireweed that covered the rolling hills. There was no more beautiful place than summer in Alaska and he dared anyone to disagree.

A moose raised its head from the kettle lake, where it stood up to its shoulders in water so clear that it held the perfect image of the mountains behind it. The movement created a waterfall over the animal's antlers and then the pristine image of the ungulate consuming an entire mouthful of fresh sedges it had retrieved from the bottom of the pond.

In the fall he would hunt for moose, perhaps even for this same animal, but who knew, there were thousands. But for now, he respected its life in the wild and gave thanks for the nourishment that fed it and had allowed it to grow into the magnificent creature it was.

He felt the train slow down. Strange, being they were only a few miles from where they had boarded. Then he felt a jolt and heard the screaming sound of the brakes trying to engage and smelled the acrid smell of the heat as the train skidded along the rails before finally coming to a halt.

Like everyone else on board, he craned to see what was happening, catching a glimpse of a lone figure climbing aboard the train and then taking a seat several seats ahead of where he sat. The man carried only a small leather bag from which he removed a leather-bound journal and began to write.

Strange that someone would be out here some 20 or so miles from any known place of habitation. As Rudy looked again out the window, he could see a tiny cabin off in the distance and assumed that the man had come from there. He had never noticed the cabin before until now.

Emma stirred beside him and rubbed her eyes.

"Are we there already?" she asked.

"No. We stopped to pick up a passenger," Rudy answered. "That man sitting about five rows ahead."

"Oh," she answered. "Amazing that they would stop an entire train for just one person. Amazing and also reassuring."

When the train stopped later in Skagway, everyone but the man got off. Emma and Rudy watched while several people boarded the train just before it pulled out of the station heading for Whitehorse.

"Not every day you carry an up and coming new poet," they heard one porter say to another. "No, sir, it just doesn't happen every day."

Emma smiled as Rudy offered to carry her bag.

"I guess we can use our imagination about who it might have been," he laughed.

But Emma wasn't listening and was instead preoccupied with wondering just where she had stashed that treasured book of Robert Service poems—just in case the poet the porters referred to had, as she suspected, been him.

CHAPTER TWENTY-TWO

WITH AN "X"

"So, you are a student of poetry," Rudy said as he walked Emma to her apartment at the Yangs'.

"It's just that this man, this Robert Service, seems somehow to speak the language of both reason and the absurd, of both trust and betrayal. Perhaps you've read his work?"

Rudy blushed and looked away, not telling Emma that except for the basics that allowed him to do his job, he could not read or write. Even his own signature was marked with an "X" and his measurements copied from those engraved on his scales and marked with seals stamped with a set of brass markers his father's father had forged.

But despite his inability to read, he held a healthy appreciation for both poetry and prose, both of which his wife had spent most every night reading to him in front of the fireplace inside their cabin.

He had always been able to perform his duties as assayer with impeccable accuracy, having learned the skills of his trade from his own father, who had learned them from his father before him.

It was only a few days later that Emma learned firsthand of Rudy's inability to read or write, when in front of a notary he used his customary "X" and a seal to mark the papers transferring Hans Derrkstad's cabin.

Unsure of how to broach the subject with him, or if it was even any of her concern, she said nothing until a couple of days later when they met at the general store to purchase firearms for her residence at *Sven's Crossing*.

The day was one of those rare very hot days when the sky was as deep a blue as one could imagine, and the ambient temperature reminded a person of what it must be like to live on the equator.

"Perhaps you won't mind if we stop and have a cold beverage next door," she said.

"Why, no," Rudy answered. "I could use some refreshment myself."

"You may be interested in knowing that I found my book of poems," she began.

"It was right under my nose. So silly of me to have overlooked it."

Rudy nodded and took a sip of ginger ale.

"We are, indeed, fortunate to have a soda fountain this far north, Miss Emma," he said. "Ahhh, so very, very fortunate."

"If you will forgive me for being presumptuous," Emma said, "I would be so honored to hear your opinion of this most recent, and to me somewhat mysterious poem by our beloved Mr. Service."

Rudy took a long swig of his ginger ale before standing.

"As much as I would like to indulge your penchant for pursuing every detail of the writings of Mr. Service," he said, "If we are to purchase firearms, we truly should move to the general store and begin."

'Well, perhaps just this one very tricky line?" she persisted.

"I'm sorry . . ." Rudy said, flushing. "I'm sorry, Miss Emma, but my reading skills are poor."

Rudy got up and strode out the door, paying for both their drinks on the way out.

"I'm so sorry, Mr. Munson . . . Rudy," she said. "I only pursued this as a test to see if I was right about your inability to read, but now I've overstepped the boundaries of both friendship and decency and embarrassed you when you've been nothing but helpful and kind to me since our first meeting. Please, Mr. Munson, please forgive me."

Rudy stopped and turned to Emma.

"I love poetry as much as you do, Miss Emma, and I miss the sound of my sweet wife Lillian's voice as she read to me each evening. The truth of the matter is that I began working at the age of twelve and was never afforded the opportunity to receive formal schooling. "

Now it was Emma's turn to blush.

"But despite the fact that the income I brought to my family after my father's unfortunate accident brought me personal reward and occupational skills that serve me well to this day, until now that very work has kept me from pursuing the education I so desperately desire."

Silently, Emma followed Rudy inside and stood as he bartered with the proprietor for the purchase of a rifle, a shotgun, and a pistol.

"Try these," he said, handing each firearm to her in turn and asking her opinion about its feel.

"I'm embarrassed to say that I know nothing about firearms or how they would normally feel," she said.

"Well, then I'll help you decide," Rudy said, "And then I'll teach you to use them."

Emma blushed again.

"Then I, sir, will in return teach you to read."

CHAPTER TWENTY-THREE
LETTER FROM WEMBLEY

On the second to the last day in July, 1912 a letter from Britain arrived for Emma.

My Dearest Mrs. Emma Brownston,

On behalf of my wife, Miriam, and myself, I pray you are well and extend our most sincere greetings to you in Alaska.

As I wrote in my quarterly report just prior to you sailing north, Lavender Blue *has been enjoying the largest boon in her history, with large quantities of plants, flowers, and oils being purchased by the crown. Indeed, our new and most royal King George V and the Queen Consort, Mary, have personally expressed their admiration for the quality of lavender and lavender products that we supply.*

As you can imagine, this notoriety on top of Britain's own booming economy has allowed us to increase production beyond our wildest imaginations.

Unfortunately, there are now signs that this burgeoning interest in lavender is about to suffer in the pattern of so many other industries in our beloved homeland due to what the government and those reporting on the government are dubbing The Great Unrest.

Currently, our largest failure with distribution is coming at the hands of striking ship and railroad employees, who are engaging in mass strikes for higher wages and less control from both government and their employers. The strikes are of such impact on our economy, that the government has begun deploying the military to return people to their places of employ.

Adding to this impending chaos is the growing presence of the women's suffragette movement and mass protests wrought by children—yes, I dare say, children—who have taken to the streets in what is becoming one of the largest periods of social unrest in the history of our nation.

In advance of this unprecedented downturn in our economy, I have taken the liberty of decreasing production at Lavender Blue *beginning with the culling of plants by 30% last spring. I have also overseen innovative new methods of long-term storage and preservation of our product line, as I await further instructions from you as to how to proceed.*

Should the situation here in Britain continue to escalate, I will proceed with my best-engineered plan—a plan that has not yet been born.

Please know that my loyalty to both you and to Lavender Blue *is unconditional and that it is my opinion, based on years of service to this estate, that we will easily weather any temporary downturn in the economy in order to both protect and preserve our assets for the future.*

As it will take another thirty-odd days for your reply to reach me from Alaska, I urge you to respond at your most urgent convenience.

Indebted in service always,
James Knox
Overseer
Lavender Blue Estates
Wembley, Borough of Brent
England

Emma read the letter again and then once more before carefully folding it and placing it inside the book of poems she carried with her at all times.

She had run into some of the suffragettes in New York and had felt lucky to have escaped their grasp, for they were women more outspoken and less beholding of true femininity than was her personal ideal, and although their cause did bear righteous intent, it was, instead, their manner in presenting it that she found distasteful.

As for the Great Unrest, she would have to take James Knox at his word about its impact on the fabric of Britain's economy.

As she reached to quell the night lamp beside her bed, she touched the letter again before falling into fitful sleep.

CHAPTER TWENTY-FOUR

GILDA

Emma was both timely and brief in her response to James Knox, telling him that she was fully confident in his ability to protect not only *Lavender Blue,* but her interest in it as well. She informed him that she had fallen into an exciting and unexpected situation in Alaska and that although her original plan had been to return to England before fall, she would now be staying in Alaska for approximately the next year and had filed the necessary paperwork to do so.

> . . .*With utmost affection and trust cast upon you, Miriam, and your family,*
>   *I remain yours truly,*
>   *Emma.*

She had no sooner left Chan Yang's apartment than she heard the clap of thunder and decided to take a shortcut to the post office through the alley behind the boarding house. Although thunder was uncommon in much of Alaska, during exceptionally hot days, thunderstorms sometimes occurred and often sparked wildfires in some of Alaska's millions of acres of forest.

Normally she avoided the alley as it was narrow, unsightly, and frequented by unsavory characters of all types, but it was midday and she needed the letter to go out and so she packed the pistol that Rudy had been teaching her to shoot, grabbed an umbrella and began to walk.

She was halfway past the first boarding house and approaching the second when she spotted a woman leaning out the back door, puffing on a cigar. Emma tried not to stare at the rumpled-appearing woman, who had her flaming red hair pinned haphazardly atop her head, and whose unbuttoned dress left her underbodice in full view.

"Well now, imagine that, Sylvia," she called to someone inside the boarding house. "Looks like we found respectability, what with the likes of miss prim and proper walking amongst us."

Emma deftly slipped her right hand into the pocket in her skirt and grasped her pistol, while holding her umbrella in her left hand. The letter remained secure in an inside pocket of her tightly buttoned jacket.

"Afternoon," Emma said as she walked by, but she was stopped abruptly when the woman placed a hand on her elbow and pulled her aside.

"Sylvia!" the woman said loudly. "Oh, forget her," she added. "Probably catching a nap since she was up most of the night." The woman laughed a raucous laugh that made Emma uncomfortable. It was clear that the stranger was a woman of ill repute. Skagway and the entire area housed more than their share of these bordello workers, as most men came up to prospect alone and most women chose to remain well away from the bawdy frontier land that was preterritorial Alaska.

"Please remove your hand from my arm," Emma said. "If it's money you want, well . . ."

"You talk funny," the woman said. "Sylvia! You gotta listen to this."

"I'm sorry you find my speech pattern offensive," Emma replied, "but it is the only way I know to speak."

"Well . . . yeah . . . well, I s'pose," the woman said, taking another puff on her stogie.

"So, is your intent to rob me?" Emma asked.

The woman unpinned her hair and then tossed it atop her head again, resecuring it with a giant hairpin.

"Hey, just a falutin' minute here. I might be a—shall we say lady of the night, but I sure ain't no thief."

Emma looked down at her feet.

"I'm sorry," she said, "I spoke harshly with no reason. My name is Emma. Emma Brownston."

"Yeah, well they call me Gilda," the woman said. "Hey! You look like one of them suffragettes I been hearin' about. You a suffragette?"

"No, I am not!" Emma said indignantly.

"Well, I respect that!" Gilda said. "Some of us girls know how to get our way without carrying signs and spittin' in the faces of men."

Emma did not respond.

"Well, you seem decent enough of a person," Gilda said, eyeing Emma from head to toe, "and I suppose I oughta let you on with your business of the day."

"Yes, I'm off to mail a letter," Emma said. "If our visit here is finished, then I beg your pardon, but I must be on my way."

"Sure. Yeah! Stop by anytime," Gilda said.

Emma heard the door close as Gilda went back inside. Had she been lucky or did Gilda seem almost like a decent kind of person? Well, she wouldn't dare to second-guess the inner makings of a brothel worker, but Gilda did not seem that scary once you broke through her gruff surface.

She reached the post office just in time for the letter to go out on the afternoon train and then hurriedly walked back home, this time taking the main street and walking mostly on the covered boardwalks to avoid the sprinkles of rain that were just beginning to fall, as well as Gilda or any of her friends.

CHAPTER TWENTY-FIVE

YOUR KEY

The following week, Emma retrieved her trunks from storage and with the help of Rudy, moved them by train up to *Arctic White*. By the end of the week she had finished cleaning her apartment and had just finished walking around the building to turn in her key when she heard Chan Yang yelling at someone in the laundry.

"You got lots of nerve, woman. Come here with dirt from brothel and want to dirty my laundry."

"You saying my money's no good," a woman's voice said. "Then how about some solid gold nuggets?"

Was that Gilda?

"You leave now!" Chan Yang said loudly. "Take your gold and your dirty money away and you no come back! Hear?"

Emma retreated and walked away from the laundry towards town. Moments later she saw Gilda heading in her direction. She thought of turning into one of the many stores that lined the street, but didn't. Instead, she slowed her pace and then turned, pretending to look for something.

The voice she heard had indeed been Gilda's, but the woman she saw now bore little resemblance to the brassy harlot who had recently stopped her in the alley. Gilda's red hair was pulled back into a sleek chignon, which was mostly covered with a headscarf she wore tied at the nape of her neck. She wore a high-buttoned blouse, a rather simple skirt, and was carrying a satchel of laundry in both arms.

"Gilda?" Emma said, catching the woman by surprise. "You may remember me, Emma."

Gilda lowered her head and kept walking, but not before Emma saw tears trickling down her cheeks.

This time it was Emma who took Gilda by the elbow, slowing her down to a stop and turning her so they faced each other. Gone was the overpowering smell of smoke and alcohol that had surrounded their first meeting.

"I heard Chan Yang," Emma said softly. "I wasn't trying to eavesdrop, but when I came around the corner, I heard."

"That's all right," Gilda said. "Happens all the time to people like me."

Suddenly Gilda was crying, so Emma led her to a bench, where they sat in the overlapping shadows of two buildings.

"My father was a doctor," Gilda said. "But he died when I was eight. Typhoid. My mother died right after. Same thing. Typhoid."

Emma listened, nodding, but saying nothing.

"I got sent to live with an aunt, but her husband was a drunk and made her send me to work. He did some other things to me that my aunt never knew about, so when I was twelve, I ran away."

Emma took the laundry bag from Gilda's lap and set it on the ground.

"They caught me and sent me back there twice, but then I met a guy who said I could make a lot of money up in Alaska helping miners, so I took the steamship ticket he offered me, lied about my age, and came here. By then I was sixteen."

"I see," Emma said softly.

"Turns out the man who bought my ticket pretty much paid for my future, 'cause when I got up here, he took me to the brothel and put me in the hands of the madam there, who managed to keep me fully employed just about every day, all day."

Gilda dried her eyes and looked directly at Emma.

"By then I had no choices . . ."

Emma sat with Gilda until the sun began to set and then stood, took her laundry bag and handed Gilda a clean hanky from her pocket.

"I'll be leaving Skagway for a while come morning, but I'll leave these on the stoop outside your door before I go."

Emma took the bag of laundry from Gilda, then stood and walked away, going directly to Yang's laundry, where she personally washed and ironed all of Gilda's clothes and packed them neatly into the freshly washed canvas bag.

She slept soundly her last night in Chan Yang's apartment, getting up early to find the woman in her laundry, where she turned in her key. Then, without saying a word, she walked out the door, turned down the alley and left the bag of clean clothes on Gilda's stoop, before heading to the train station, where she caught the eight-thirty train to *Sven's Crossing*.

Rudy had taught her well in the use of firearms and she was ready—as ready as she had ever been in her life, a life now marked by standing tall and moving forward in search of harmony with this wild land they called Alaska.

CHAPTER TWENTY-SIX

SURPRISE ON THE TRAIL

By now Emma was well versed in the ways of travel by rail, so she leaned back and relaxed with her book of poems as the train made its way to the drop-off near *Sven's Crossing*. No matter how many times she read them, she never tired of reading the works of Robert Service. To the contrary, she seemed to get more out of his writing with each reading.

She had used this very book to teach Rudolph Munson to read and he had been both a willing and a diligent student. It came as no surprise that he was already able to read most of the poems in her book. She had also been working with him on writing. After only three weeks, he now knew how to write each letter of the alphabet in both cursive and print and knew how to sign his name. Although he still had problems with spelling and grammar, he had made enough progress to at least present his business face in a more professional manner.

For some reason he had learned numbers and math early on and this had not only served him well, but most likely had allowed him to function with credibility in his work as an assayer.

As promised, he had taught Emma to use firearms, stating his satisfaction that she had enough knowledge and expertise to function in an emergency, even while insisting that she not become overconfident or brash in her handling of such dangerous weapons.

It was late morning when Emma saw the junction for *Sven's Crossing* and flagged the train to stop. Grabbing her bag and her book, she stepped off into the light of a bright sunny day and began to walk the mile or so to *Arctic White*. The day was quiet, making it easy to immerse herself in nature's glory until she was suddenly startled by the sound of a rustle nearby, and then a popping or clicking noise.

She stopped and waited, then heard it again, backing steadily away from the unfamiliar sound. The noise frightened her and put her on edge. Something told her to reach for her pistol, so she did, pulling it out of her bag and cocking it just in case. In the sun she waited, afraid to move and afraid to relax. She didn't need to wait for long, for there on the trail about thirty feet ahead was a large, black animal that she could only surmise must be one of the bears she had heard so much about.

A rustle of the leaves signaled the onset of the wind, and within minutes a stiff breeze began blowing her way. She would later learn that this was a best-case scenario for this situation, for it blew her scent away from the bear and likely prevented a closer encounter or even an attack.

After what seemed like an eternity in time, the bear stood up, sniffed the air, and then moved away from her along the trail. She watched as it lumbered along before veering away from the direction of *Sven's Crossing*. Even so, she stood there almost till dusk before slowly moving ahead, making sure to whistle and sing like Rudy had taught her to do.

She sang the British National Anthem, she sang songs of her childhood, and she sang a couple of more songs that she made up as she went along. By the time she reached *Arctic White* she was both hoarse and exhausted.

There were lights on in Sven's cabin, but no one came out, so she used the key Rudy had given her and lifted the wooden bolts that let her in the cabin, relieved that it felt like home.

She had spent the last several trips arranging her few things inside and now *Arctic White* felt at least somewhat familiar. She had brought one large woolen rug from England, an old favorite that carried a floral pattern of lavender plants in bloom. It was beautiful against the wooden floor and in front of the stone fireplace in the living room. It had been her one indulgence in deciding which of her personal items warranted the time and expense to ship to Alaska. Just seeing it eased much of the tension she had felt from seeing her first bear.

She had no sooner lit her lantern than she heard a shot, followed quickly by another. Moving to the floor, she lay on the rug and waited, but heard nothing more, so she sat on a bench and waited before loading some wood in the fireplace.

A knock on the door was quickly followed by the voice of Sven Bjorstad.

"Emma, it's safe to open your door. It's Sven."

When she did open the huge wooden door, Sven Bjorstad stood there with his rifle at his side.

"I know you must have heard the shots and you should know that I took down a bear about a hundred yards from this cabin."

Emma's mouth dropped open at the news.

"Was it large and black?"

"It was," Sven answered. "Are you telling me you saw it?"

"Yes, when I got off the train."

She proceeded to tell him the story of her encounter.

Sven wiped his brow and looked at her.

"It's been raiding my chickens for the last week," he said, "but I figured I ran it off. When it came at me on the way back from Doc's cabin, I put it down for good. I'll be skinning it and salvaging the meat most of tonight, but first I want to hook up my horse and drag it to my cabin. Just wanted to alert you to the commotion."

"Thank you, Sven," Emma said.

"You were lucky today," he told her. "We're going to need to talk."

Emma closed the door and secured the latch, not sure what Sven had in mind about talking, but she suspected it had to do with bears and about her ability to survive their presence should she ever find herself in a similar situation again.

CHAPTER TWENTY-SEVEN

HELEN LAUREL AUSTIN

It took about three days, but Sven did stop by to talk with her about the bear and help her come up with a plan for future encounters.

". . . and they *will* happen," he said.

The distance from the train tracks was about a mile, a rather long distance to walk alone in the wilderness. The path was not heavily traveled either, which added to the danger.

"Usually the dogs tell me when there is an animal or person around," Sven said, "and I usually take our housedog, Jake, with me when I leave the homestead. Jake alerts me without making a sound."

Emma listened as Sven talked, nodding periodically and without ever taking her eyes off him. When he had finished, she thanked him for sharing his advice and told him she looked forward to the three wooden shelters that he would be building along the path.

"I just feel better about that with you being a lady . . ." he said.

He had also urged her to practice her firearm skills regularly and to even consider getting a dog of her own, which he assured her he would help train and bond with the other dogs at *Sven's Crossing*.

"Just know that a dog can be a double-edged sword," he told Emma. "It can run a bear either towards or away from you, depending on the bear and its encounter with the dog. Lots of variables there."

As the first frosts of September appeared, Emma began making lists so that her trips into Skagway would be as productive as possible. She had already arranged for Sven to chop and supply her wood, and had purchased a large kettle that could be hung on an iron hook inside the fireplace. She would use it for melting snow for water if her plumbing system should freeze and for making soups, stews, and whatever else she could conjure up.

She hadn't seen Rudolph Munson in a month or more, so on her last trip into town she made a point of stopping in at the assay office to pay her respects. Instead of Rudy standing behind the counter, though, she saw the back of a woman clad in one of the sensible dresses of the day and with her brown hair pulled up neatly atop her head.

"Excuse me," Emma said with her English accent instantly revealing who she was, "But might I find Mr. Munson available?"

For an uncomfortably long time, the woman didn't turn around, but when she did, Emma immediately recognized her.

"Gilda?"

"Helen Laurel Austin by birth," the woman she had known as Gilda answered. "Please call me Helen."

"So nice to see you again . . . Helen," Emma said.

"I know you're surprised," Helen said, using the modulated tone and perfect diction of a person raised to respect propriety. "But you are too classy to show it."

"I only came to visit Mr. Munson," Emma said. "But it is nice to see you well."

"He knows," Helen volunteered, as if imagining Emma's next question. "I decided that if I were to have a clean start, I would have to be honest. I mean, people talk."

"I'm not here to judge," Emma answered.

"I needed to find work and Ru—Mr. Munson—took me in. So far, I believe it has given him the freedom to travel more freely and that is why today, you will not find him here, but up along the Yukon River hunting moose."

Emma waited before speaking, taking some time to look at some of the gold nuggets on display in the shop. When she answered, she looked squarely at Helen Austin.

"I celebrate your job advancement with you, Miss Austin, and I celebrate Mr. Munson's wisdom in hiring you. Please tell him I stopped by and will likely not return again until spring."

Emma turned and walked out the door only to be stopped by Helen calling her name.

"Mrs. Brownston. You are a true lady and you are a true friend. Thank you."

Emma smiled before continuing on her way. With the shop under control, she imagined that Rudy would more than likely find his way to *Sven's Crossing* on his way home to tell her this very news himself.

CHAPTER TWENTY-EIGHT

TAKE IT OR LEAVE IT

As she walked past the brothel, Emma could hear raucous sounds coming from the bar located at street level. She quickened her pace a bit, aware of the stares from a couple of miners who were standing on the boardwalk out front.

As she walked by, she could hear snippets of their conversation:

"Word is they're thinkin' a makin' Alaska a Territory of the United States."

"Hawww!" one of the men answered before spitting into the spittoon. "You callin' me a liar?"

"Ain't that yer a liar, more that yer daft," came the reply. "Next you'll be wearin' a petticoat with them women in white that thinks they's equal to a man."

"You callin' me a woman?"

"I'm callin' ya crazy."

Emma continued walking, making a turn around one of the buildings just in case the disagreement escalated. She had seen that happen before in the frontier where she now stood. Miners—tired, rich, drunk after having been away from the city for months on end—getting into arguments and doing stupid things.

By the time she reached Chan Yang's, she could no longer hear their voices, nor had she heard any gunfire.

"That you, Emma?" she heard a voice say.

"It me, Chan Yang."

"Afternoon, Chan Yang. I hope this beautiful day finds you and Yun Yang well."

"Apartment still empty," Chan Yang said without acknowledging Emma's greeting. "No suitable renters."

"I'm sorry," Emma replied.

"You want to rent again?"

"I have a place up at *Sven's Crossing* now," Emma answered.

"*Sven's Crossing*? Not hear of that place. Can't be much to it. You here now. Make you a good deal."

Emma smiled and started walking again.

"Need the money," Chan Yang said. "Yun Yang gone. Dead now. Happened fast. Heart."

"I'm so very sorry," Emma said, stopping and turning around. "Why I was here just a month ago and he seemed fine."

"Woke up dead," Chan Yang said. "Shock to me, too. So, you'll rent? Give you a good deal."

"I suppose it would be nice to have a place to stay here in town," Emma answered. "But I wouldn't be here often."

Chan Yang scowled as if running the numbers of profit in her head.

"I rent to you for half of before," she said.

"I couldn't possibly consider that much for as little as I'd be here," Emma answered. "And there's the question of heat and water and laundry . . ."

"Okay, Mrs. Emma. You drive hard bargain, but Chan Yang desperate. I give you for third," Chan Yang said firmly. "Final offer. Not go lower. Take or leave. "

"Well, okay, Chan Yang. I will take it and I'll pay you now for the next year's rent."

'That fine," Chan Yang answered. "Pay in gold, okay?"

"Okay," Emma answered, reaching into her bag to give partial payment to Chan Yang.

"I'll get the rest to you in the morning."

"Okay, but don't try to cheat," Chan Yang said. "I know you rich."

"You have my word," Emma said, without blinking. "And I'm sorry you lost your husband. Very sorry. He was a good man."

Emma followed Chan Yang around the building where she accepted the key. She had long ago come to terms with Chan Yang's rigid thinking and black and white view of the world.

When she got to the apartment, she could see it was mostly as she had left it. The familiarity gave her comfort. Even in one short month so much had changed. She was now a frontier woman—a pioneer, even. Then there was the change at the assay office with Gilda-now-Helen managing the shop while Rudy was away.

During that time, Yun Yang had died, Gilda had returned to respectability, and now there was even talk about Alaska joining the United States. Could she ever have foreseen this when she had decided to return to Alaska?

"By the way," Chan Yang said after knocking on the door to leave Emma some clean towels, "The boy, Lars—got a letter. He in school. Smart. Good grades. Happy. Thought you should know."

"Thank you," Emma said. "Thank you for letting me know."

CHAPTER TWENTY-NINE

MAIL

Emma left Skagway the next morning, but not before picking up her mail at the post office and also securing the rest of the payment for Chan Yang.

"I check room once a week," Chan Yang said. "Make sure okay."

Emma gave the woman a perfunctory hug and walked toward the train station while pulling a cart full of supplies. It would have been just as easy to bring a horse-drawn wagon into town, but she hadn't planned on shopping this heavily. Thankfully, the railcar attendant helped her with her bags and before the day had reached high noon, she was sitting comfortably in her seat eating lunch.

She took the bundle of mail from her bag and sorted it. There were three letters from her attorney—all routine business related to *Lavender Blue* that required her personal signature. She would complete them later and leave them with proper postage for the conductor to mail when the train returned to Skagway.

Her mail also contained a couple of letters from friends back in Wembley, friends she had known since childhood. She tucked those into her bag to read and enjoy later. Last, she found a letter from James Knox. It began with his usual professional salutation and several updates on business at *Lavender Blue*, which he described in the most positive of terms. About halfway through the letter, one comment caught her attention:

The suffragette movement is in full progress here, and although I have always supported the equality of women, I find their tactics to be both aggressive and confrontational. You can then imagine how distressing it was for me to find my own Miriam blocked from the very gates of Lavender Blue when returning from market recently, and how unsettling it is to know that I must be vigilant on her behalf for fear that they will do her harm should she not agree to march with them.

Further, there is talk of an impending miner's strike and the stockpiling of weapons as subtle signs of civil unrest have begun to manifest themselves even among our own well-paid workers.

Do be assured that I will closely monitor this movement and pray that it is only a ripple in our otherwise robust British economy and know that I remain your humble servant and loyal friend.

James Knox

Emma scowled—suffragettes in Britain, too? What was going on? Obviously, the movement was troubling James Knox or he wouldn't have bothered to mention it. She folded the letter and returned it to her bag. Later, once back in front of the fire inside *Arctic White,* she would read the letter again and respond. Her own encounter with the suffragettes in New York had been frightening, making it easy to understand James's concern for Miriam's safety. Hopefully all of this was just a small unrest.

The economy in Britain had never been more robust, so why would anyone be upset? James had said something about minimum wage concerns, but she knew they paid their workers well.

As the train rumbled to a stop, she was surprised to see Sven Bjorstad waiting with his horse and wagon.

"Daria insisted I come here to meet you," he said. "She knew your load would be heavy, that you'd be tired and that it would be late, and so I am here."

"I must remember to thank Daria personally," Emma said, "And may I tell you now that your kindness is more than appreciated as truly I am exhausted and have returned with more than I planned."

As the horse clopped along the trail, Emma took in the smell of freshness in the fall air.

"The first snow is no more than a week off," he said. "It's good you are home now and prepared."

Home, she thought. Yes, she *was* home. Would she fare well during the long winter? Had she adequately prepared? She glanced at Sven Bjorstad—at his strong hands and weathered face, and at his determined demeanor. Fortune had indeed smiled on her in the inheriting of *Arctic White,* just as it had with James and Miriam Knox at *Lavender Blue.* If someone had told her two years ago that this would be her life, she would never have believed them. "Oh, and Rudy came by," Sven said, interrupting the solitude. "He brought some moose. Sorry he missed you—that's what he told me. Anyway, moose is in my meat cache. Get any you want, whenever you want."

Emma had only seen one moose, and that had been from a distance. Still, she couldn't imagine that any meat from such a large and gangly animal would be anything she would ever try, but she thanked Sven anyway. Later she would ask him what a meat cache was and where to find it.

When they arrived at her cabin, she helped Sven carry in her supplies, then after thanking him profusely, she shut the door and thanked God for her great fortune in life.

Later that evening, she joined Sven and Daria for a moose roast at their cabin, feeling no hesitation whatsoever in telling Daria that it was the best meat she had ever eaten.

The meat cache, she learned on the way out, was halfway between the two cabins.

"But don't you be worryin' about climbin' that steep ladder," Sven said. "I don't let Daria climb it and I won't be lettin' you either. You just call me when you need some meat."

She walked back to her cabin, enjoying the brisk air and the night's darkness. Had she ever seen so many stars? And the northern lights, they were every bit as beautiful as described in many of the books she had read, and to her mind that was exceptionally beautiful indeed.

CHAPTER THIRTY

TRESPASSERS WILL BE SHOT

Not only did Emma learn to love moose, but she also learned to cook it, with moose stew being her favorite. She had never really had to cook, at least not since childhood, when she helped her mother. She found that she enjoyed it and especially liked perfecting the technique of cooking it in the hanging kettle over an open fire in the fireplace.

By December she was fully settled in and already calling herself an Alaskan. The darkness was as troublesome as it was comforting. The days were now only about two hours long with the rest of the time being dusk, dawn, and night.

At first, she had been afraid to go out in the dark, but she quickly learned that her eyes actually adjusted quite well—especially when there was snow and a bright moon reflecting off it. She also learned that on the coldest nights, when the sky was so clear you could see into infinity, the northern lights were as mesmerizing and magical as anything she could have ever imagined.

It was on one of those nights that she decided to venture a bit beyond her yard, calling Jake to her as she strapped on her snowshoes.

Sven and Daria had been very generous in offering the use of Jake when she needed a companion outdoors. And Jake had done well in protecting her, once even running off a moose that wandered too close.

She had been wise to purchase furs from the skin sewer at Hans Derrkstad's old mercantile. She had a heavy ankle-length parka with a wolf and otter ruff, sealskin mittens and covers for her mukluks. She also had a quiviut face gaiter that even covered her eyes. At sixty below, even this heavily dressed, she wouldn't be out for long.

Jake's coat was long with a thick undercoat, but he also was fitted with a sealskin coat and boots. The snow crunched and the northern lights crackled as they walked along, moving in the direction of the closest cabin, whose lights could not be seen until she had lost sight of her own.

A sharp snap pierced the air just as she saw the lights, followed quickly by another.

'Those was jest a warnin', stranger. Next one's gonna be fer real."

Emma froze and called Jake to her.

Should she respond?

She began to retreat.

"I'm sorry if I got too close. It's Emma Brownston from *Arctic White*. I'm heading back to my cabin now."

Her call was followed by silence as she continued to back slowly away from the cabin. Only when she was halfway back to *Arctic White* did she hear the sound of a door slamming shut. It felt like she couldn't breathe. Was it the cold? The quiviut gaiter? Adrenaline? All three?

Finally, she reached her cabin and went inside, stopping in the arctic entry to remove her outerwear before entering the warmth inside. She brought Jake in with her and gave him some water, which he drank heartily before taking a nap. About an hour later he scratched at the door to leave and she let him go, latching the door tightly and checking again to make sure it was secure.

Why was she still shaking? She wasn't hungry, but she ate some of the moose stew simmering over the fire in order to warm herself, and then looked out the window to make sure a lantern was lit in the window of Sven and Daria's cabin—their signal that Jake was safely inside. Later, when she did climb under her comforter in bed, she lay awake for a very long time, before finally falling asleep with the promise to never go out alone like that again.

The next morning over coffee, she told the story to Sven, who had stopped by to see why Jake had come home still wearing his sealskin coat.

"Jake came in all geared up, so I figured you two went out," he said.

Emma explained, describing in detail the sounds of the shots and the slamming door.

"I knew something like this would happen what with you bein' a cheechako and all that," Sven said.

Emma watched as he paced the room.

"You're lucky old Nate didn't shoot first and ask questions later," he said. "He's been ornerier than a bear sow with separated cubs ever since he stopped working his claim and he started holing up in that cabin drinking all winter long. Everyone here knows to stay back when he starts talking like an uneducated hick instead of the intelligent man he is."

"I only found his place by accident. I wasn't going to go far . . ."

Emma fumbled for words. She knew she had taken a huge risk in even being outdoors in this kind of cold.

"I'd head over and tell him to back off if I didn't care that much about stayin' alive," Sven said, "but when the time's right, I'll be talking to him. Meanwhile, you just stay in this cabin unless you absolutely have to be outside."

Emma nodded.

"You start getting squirrelly, then call me and I'll take you out."

"Okay," Emma promised as she walked with him to the door.

"Most women know enough to spin and weave and do women's stuff in winter," Sven said. "Maybe there's a lesson in that for you."

Maybe there was, Emma told herself. Maybe she had no business being here at all.

Chapter Thirty-One

INVITATION

Emma took the train into Skagway right before Thanksgiving. Although she had little understanding of this American holiday, Sven and Daria had invited her to participate in a community dinner to celebrate the event. Attending would be Sven and Daria, Emma, a couple of officials from the railroad and their families, another miner named Slim—if he decided to forego a trip to Skagway in order to stay—and Nate.

"Don't worry about ole Nate," Sven had told her. "He doesn't even remember that day when he confronted you."

Emma felt her shoulders tense and then relax. As scary as the encounter with Nate had been, she would be in the company of others, so why should she worry?

Staying one night in town would give her enough time to search the local shops for the right gift for her hosts and the right ingredients to use for the dessert she had promised to bring. She had already decided on a white cake with buttercream frosting on which she would place an arrangement of lavender flowers she would make from another frosting recipe James Knox's wife, Miriam, had given her.

She purchased a stemmed crystal plate that came with a glass cover. It would be perfect for the occasion. She also ordered two pairs of sealskin mittens that she would give to Daria and Sven for Christmas and arranged to have a lovely beaded tablecloth mailed to James and Miriam Knox—both made by the skin sewer and his wife at the mercantile.

As for the dinner, she purchased a set of linen napkins that had recently arrived at the mercantile and waited while they were embroidered with a fancy lavender "B" in one corner. They would be for her hosts and a very personal offering from her heart.

She had already stopped in to say hello to Chan Yang, but there was no one around, so she walked across to the boardwalk and hired a horse-drawn sleigh to take her across town to the assay office.

Rudy greeted her enthusiastically when she entered, telling her he was surprised to see her in town in the winter. When she explained about Thanksgiving, he hesitated a bit before telling her that he had been invited by Sven and Daria and would be arriving the day before Thanksgiving with a friend.

"It will be wonderful to have time for a visit," she told him, "and you and your friend are both welcome at *Arctic White*."

Rudy smiled and hugged her before stepping back.

"Before I accept, I would like your assurance that my friend is indeed welcome and need you to know that Helen and I will not require separate accommodations."

When Emma hesitated to respond, he added, "I know you have met Helen and that you know of her past, just as I know you will not judge our happy engagement."

"Engagement?" Emma asked.

"Yes, Emma, we are engaged. I know it seems abrupt, but with Helen I have found renewal and hope and she has expressed an equal sentiment to me."

"Then my most fervent congratulations," Emma said, feigning exuberance. "I shall prepare for your warmly anticipated visit."

After climbing back into the sleigh for the trip back to her apartment, Emma turned to look back at Rudy, who had resumed tinkering around the shop. She had sensed a newfound contentment in his demeanor and smiled when recalling the somewhat awkward way he had broken the news.

It would be a bit uncomfortable for her at the house when they arrived, but hopefully Helen had succeeded in permanently putting her past behind her enough to truly embrace a man like Rudy, and hopefully Rudy would not in his loneliness have given his heart too freely.

As she settled back into her seat on the train ride home, she found herself reflecting on her life. Today seemed so far away from her long years with Hershell Brownston.

Then, she never would have imagined traveling, let alone living in the wilds of Alaska, nor would she have dreamed of meeting all the new people in her life—friends like Hans Derrkstad and Lars, Yun and Chan Yang, Rudolph Munson, Sven, Daria, and Gilda-now-Helen.

As she looked at the scenery flashing by, her past in England seemed an entire lifetime ago. She settled back into her seat, letting the thoughts run through her head. Moments later, she heard the scream of the train's brakes and felt the car wobble a bit as they came to a stop.

"Avalanche on the tracks," the porter said. "We'll be supplying blankets and firing the engine to provide heat, but looks like we'll be here till morning when they can get us dug out."

Thankfully, Emma had brought her warm fur coat and boots. Sven had insisted early on that she learn to always be prepared when traveling. She had no sooner retrieved her bag and begun to dress more warmly than she saw a familiar face two rows behind her.

Besides herself and a smattering of other passengers, he was the only other traveler on the train. She pulled out her book of Robert Service poems and began to read. A short while later, she heard the person behind her call.

"Hey, ma'am. Now ya wouldn't be the newcomer that swore to Sven Bjorstad I chased ya with ma gun now, would ya?"

Emma tensed and kept reading, looking up briefly to make sure the porter was nearby.

"Hell, I don't blame ya fer bein' scared. Even I'm scared a me sometimes." Since it appeared that the man would not relent, Emma summoned all her strength and stood, walking back to him and extending her hand, trying to ignore the stench of alcohol surrounding him.

"I'm Emma Brownston of *Arctic White*," she said. "And you would be?"

The stranger stood, removing his hat and slicking back his red hair with one hand, while awkwardly smoothing his bushy red beard with the other before answering.

"Nate Dryson, ma'am. Pleasure."

"Well, pleased to meet you Mr. Dryson and although you do bear some resemblance to the man who shot at me, it was in fact dark, and therefore I cannot in good conscience swear it was you. Further, in meeting you, I feel some reassurance that you are a man whom, if in fact you were the person I should fear, I find utterly lacking in threatening demeanor at present."

Nate scratched his head and sat down.

"Now that's a damn mouthful," he said looking straight at Emma, suddenly speaking with a modicum of intelligence. "I can't say as I've heard a woman talk like you in the full entirety of my existence."

"I simply said that I cannot prove it was you who threatened me and that I don't fear you now," Emma told him.

"I see," Nate answered, again scratching his head.

"Will you be warm enough?" Emma asked, "because you seem to have little with you and I brought an extra blanket."

Nate squinted before accepting.

"Yer kindness overwhelms me," he chuckled. "But I've got something else to keep me warm."

Emma watched as Nate patted his breast pocket while he spoke before returning to her seat and reading until her eyes fluttered closed. The train was warmer than one would have expected, although the stiffness of the bench seat gave little comfort. Still, like all the others, she stretched out on her side and prepared to sleep, only to be awakened by the sound of Nate's voice.

"I don't tell this ta too many people," Nate said. "Can't trust most of 'em, but I like you."

Emma sat up and looked at him.

"There's no need to explain and it is late," she said.

"Ya see, I got me a job no matter what the pundits say," Nate said, as if he hadn't heard her. "And that job is death."

"Death?" Emma said, now fully awake.

"Ya heard me right—death. And it's a full-timer all right. Death. That's what I do. Takes all my time thinkin' bout it, plannin' it, dreadin' it, gettin' ready for it, and otherwise wrappin' my very existence around it."

"Why are you telling me this, Mr. Nate?" Emma said, indignantly "Are you trying to scare me? Because I am not afraid."

"Yeah, maybe I am," Nate laughed in an eerie kind of way that made Emma cast a glance at the porter.

"Are you okay, ma'am?" the porter asked. "Ole Nate here botherin' you?"

Emma didn't answer.

She watched the porter approach Nate.

"Dan'l, you can close your eyes in the warm comfort of this car, or you can sleep outside with the wolves for all I care, but there will be no more bothering the other passengers and you know I do mean business, my friend."

Nate began to stand before sitting back down.

"Any other circumstances and you wouldn't be getting' away with tellin' me what ta do or with callin' me Dan'l," Nate said, his words beginning to slur.

"Well, these circumstances, being what they are, direct me to tell you exactly what to do," the porter said. "And if I choose to call you Dan'l, then that's only because that's your given name and just about anyone aside from this tender lady here knows it."

"My apologies, ma'am," Nate said, laying out on his bench and pulling the blanket tightly around him.

Within minutes he was snoring. Annoying as it was, at least it provided some assurance to Emma that Nate—or Daniel, if that was his real name—wouldn't be bothering her for a while.

CHAPTER THIRTY-TWO

DAN'L

Emma found herself unable to sleep, a situation made worse by the sound of something falling to the floor behind her. When she looked back, she saw what looked like a flask lying on the floor right below Nate's outstretched arm.

Sven had mentioned the drinking and Nate's propensity to become hostile when he was drunk. Perhaps that explained his odd rant about death. But what about the fact that the porter had called him Dan'l and why did she even care?

She sat up on the bench and looked outside. Darkness surrounded the stranded train and a strong wind had begun to blow. The sky, although filled with stars, had only the sliver of a moon casting light. Then she saw them emerge—the Northern Lights. They began with a small upward steak of green rising from behind a mountain and into the sky.

Within minutes, the wall of vertical streaks began to make its way across the sky like a winding band of color. Soon, another band of pink appeared behind the green, expanding even farther up into the sky until, finally, the entire night was filled with the undulating ribbons of color.

Emma watched, so mesmerized that she failed to hear the sound of the porter approach.

"May I sit down?"

His voice startled her as she jumped and turned to face him.

"Of course. Is something wrong?" she asked.

"I saw you awake and suspected that Dan'l had caused you to feel unsure of your safety. With your permission, I would like to tell you more about him with the intent of engaging your understanding."

Emma nodded and settled into her seat.

"Dan'l had a claim not far from the Yukon River that some say was one of the biggest veins of gold anyone had ever found," the porter began. "For years he would come into Skagway, usually by this very train, and bring his poke into the assay office for quantifying. The assayer will verify that if you ask him."

Emma turned to face the porter.

"Yes, okay. I do know the assayer, Mr. Munson."

"Dan'l had a partner named Nate Dryson. The two of them . . ."

Emma listened as the porter continued the story of how Daniel and his partner had not only worked one of the most lucrative claims in the gold rush, but had done so without the acrimony that so often marked partnerships during the grab for gold.

"They were as close as two brothers," the porter continued. "Some say the relationship was as unbreakable as any they had ever seen."

Emma sat transfixed as the porter continued with the story, explaining how Daniel would work the claim while Nate brought the gold into town and vice versa. He shared with her how this went on for several years, their routine becoming so steadfast that a person could set their calendar on the comings and goings of the two miners.

He mentioned how occasionally the two men would come into Skagway at the same time—like to celebrate a birthday—but never for very long so as not to leave their claim unattended.

"As far as I heard it told, no one ever violated their claim or even tried—that's how respected the two of them were.

"It happened one July, after one of those birthday trips into Skagway. The way the story goes is that Dan'l and Nate got back to their claim only to find that a landslide had fallen over their camp and blocked just about all access to their claim.

"Undeterred, the two men worked day and night to find a way through the rubble and had just broken through when another landslide occurred, this time washing Nate with it under a mountain of rock.

"They say that Dan'l tried to dig him out for three days before collapsing from exhaustion. A couple of neighboring miners found him while passing through and they, too, tried to move enough rock to find Nate, but to no avail.

"Finally, knowing he was lost forever, Dan'l gave up and returned to Skagway with the news."

Emma could not disguise her sorrow at the sadness of the story and shook her head slowly in response.

"Dan'l was already one of the richest miners in Skagway history and could easily have taken his gold and carved out a lucrative lifestyle for himself just about anywhere he chose, but instead, he bought a piece of land up in *Sven's Crossing*, put up a quick cabin there, and moved in—declining help from everyone who offered, and even running them off with threats and shots fired in the air."

"And, then?" Emma asked.

"Then what happened is mostly what you're seeing now. On the few occasions when Dan'l did come into town or interact with Sven Bjorstad or any of the other locals in *Sven's Crossing*, he was surly and argumentative.

"More often than not he was drunk or talking about getting drunk, and it was during these interactions that he began spewing his rhetoric about death.

"Most everyone accepted that Dan'l had gone over the edge after watching his friend die, and after a time, most stopped trying to engage him. Things steadily deteriorated, with Dan'l taking to calling himself Nate and arguing with anyone who dared say otherwise."

"It's almost like he wished he could have traded places with the real Nate," Emma said. "As if he felt guilty for having survived."

"Exactly," the porter said. "And so now, some seven or eight years later, we are witness to the once thriving Dan'l we see here."

The porter glanced back at Nate and slowly shook his head.

"It's a sad story for sure, and made even sadder by the fact that some of us knew Dan'l at his finest. Mostly, though, mostly we now just try to keep him out of trouble and let him live out his life. Can't change a man that's hell-bent on self-destruction, you know. No sirree, much as we wish—as I wish—something could save old Dan'l, well . . ."

Emma looked back at Dan'l. Little did he resemble a once thriving and successful man. She watched as he snorted and rolled over, pulling the blanket up closer to him.

"Thanks for sharing this story with me," she said to the porter. "There is power in understanding and in understanding, there is hope."

CHAPTER THIRTY-THREE
HOME

As things turned out, the avalanche-clearing special engine arrived from Whitehorse the next morning, but the job of clearing the mound of hard-packed snow was determined to be bigger than expected, so the passengers were led around the toe of the avalanche to the other side, where they boarded a caboose attached to the second engine and were ferried to *Sven's Crossing* some ten miles up the tracks. Their supplies, though, would have to wait. All that could not be carried would be delivered in two days by a special agent for the railroad, who would wire ahead to *Sven's Crossing* so that folks could meet him at the tracks.

Most passengers were bound for Whitehorse and were met by a third engine that took them to their destination, after which the second engine then returned to the avalanche to help the first.

Emma hoisted her bags, one on each shoulder, and began the walk to *Arctic White,* while Nate lagged sleepily behind her.

"A gentleman would surely offer to assist," she said, turning to face him.

Nate spat in the snow and moved towards her, taking one bag from her shoulder and hoisting it onto his own.

"I don't drink as much as they say," he said, "but when I do, I do."

"Your drinking is your business, Mr. Dryson. As much as I appreciate your less than willing assistance, I am, in fact grateful for the help as I am not able to carry these bags alone."

Daniel looked at the ground.

"I suppose I should apologize," he said. "Danged headache is rough. Thirsty."

Emma did not respond.

"Oh, so yer thinkin' I got what I deserved, are ya?"

Emma walked faster.

"Don't answer, then, but I'll be bringin' ya somethin' to yer cabin to atone soon as I sleep a night or two," Daniel said.

Emma stopped and turned to face him.

"You and all who live in *Sven's Crossing* are welcome at my cabin at any time, but I must warn you Mr. Dryson, that should you ever arrive at my door smelling of the spirits of alcohol, I will meet you with my revolver, greet you with one warning shot into the air, and then plant the next shot into parts that a lady would not choose to identify out loud."

"Yes, ma'am," Nate answered.

"And although I may be new to firearms, I am told that my aim is precise and that I have impressed my teachers with my accuracy," she added for emphasis, "so consider that you have not only been warned, but promised, for I am a woman of my word."

Nate stared sheepishly at the ground. Never before had a woman spoken to him in this way, at least, not since his fiancée had run off with a friend on learning they would be living in Alaska.

"I'll take those now. Thank you for your assistance," she said, taking her bags and setting them before her cabin. "Thank goodness Sven thought to pull a beam across this snow and make a trail for our convenience."

"Ya," Daniel said.

"Good day, then, Mr. Dryson."

"Ma'am," Daniel answered as he began to move on.

Emma watched him as he walked away. He was amazingly docile for a man who had displayed such orneriness. It was obvious that he was mourning something in life and it was equally obvious that he was having trouble doing so alone.

"I hope to see you at Thanksgiving dinner, Daniel," she called to him.

She watched as his pace slowed and his shoulders squared before moving on. She tensed, wondering what he might do with her having used his rightful name, but by the time she had taken her bags inside he had gone out of sight.

After stoking the fire, she set her bags aside for the night. Tomorrow she would go through her purchases, but for tonight, all she wanted to do was to eat something, remove her boots, and get some sleep.

There was preciously little to eat, but she did manage to find some cheese and some old bread. Tomorrow she would cook a pot of moose stew—her new favorite, and then she would make the cake for the big dinner now only two days away. She had been fortunate in being able to carry the crystal plate and cake-making ingredients with her from the train. Hopefully, the rest of the gifts would arrive soon.

She fell asleep to the sound of howling wolves and never saw the aurora appear outside her window. It must have been magical, because her sleep was deep and satisfying—so much so that she slept in an entire hour later than usual.

With the morning as bright as an Arctic winter's day could be, she woke up refreshed and ready to start her day. *Arctic White* was indeed home, and a home like none other she had ever known before.

CHAPTER THIRTY-FOUR
THANKSGIVING

Thanksgiving 1912 in *Sven's Crossing* turned out to be one of the best times Emma had ever known. Everyone was there—Rudy and Helen (who had arrived just that morning), Sven and Daria, Emma, and a couple of railroad officials, who had been dropped off by the train to Whitehorse and would be picked up later that afternoon as it traveled back to Skagway. Also, there was the driver of the mail sled and his team, all of whom were welcomed and invited to stay.

It had been several weeks since the dog-team-driven mail sled had come to *Sven's Crossing*, but with Christmas just around the corner and Thanksgiving dinner on the table, the sled had arrived with the driver promising at least one more delivery before Christmas.

No one had expected Nate to be there, and so he wasn't missed. Still, Emma did wonder at one point if he might just wander in, even suggesting to Daria that someone take him a plate of food.

"I'll be danged if . . ." Sven told his wife.

"But it's Thanksgiving," Emma and Daria had both replied, and thus he had agreed.

Since Rudy and Helen had come in later than expected due to the avalanche delaying their train, they would not need to stay with Emma and would be heading back to Skagway that evening on a special train that was stopping for the railroad executives. Otherwise, it would be two weeks before the next train.

Emma made it a point to sit with them; after all, Rudy had been instrumental in helping her find her new home and Helen had left her somewhere between happy and intrigued about what the former brothel worker's future might hold. The two did seem happy, interacting comfortably and with an undercurrent of tenderness that gave Emma hope their love was real.

"It's you we have to thank for this wonderful moose," Emma said to Rudy.

Rudy nodded and smiled.

"I'm sorry I missed your visit when you brought it by," she continued.

"Your cake is lovely," Helen told Emma. "It reminds me of some my parents brought home from our finest bakery back east when I was a child."

Only later, when the men were busy talking about hunting and mining did Emma have a moment alone with Helen.

"I'm sorry you were unable to stay longer," Emma began.

"I know you must be wondering . . ." Helen said.

"Wondering?"

"About Rudy and me," Helen answered.

Emma looked at her feet. Helen had definitely brought up the obvious, but even so, what business of hers was their relationship? She was spared from answering when Rudy came walking up.

"Did you ask her?" he said to Helen, who shook her head as if wanting him to stop.

"What?" Rudy said, not picking up her cue. "You know, about the cake?"

"I'm afraid we hadn't quite gotten there," Helen said.

"I think my lovely bride-to-be might be too shy to ask you herself," Rudy laughed. "We were wondering if you would do us the honor of making a cake for our wedding in late April?"

CHAPTER THIRTY-FIVE

NO ONE TO KNIT AND CROCHET

So much had happened since Emma's move back to Alaska. People who two years ago had been strangers to her, were now friends. Some of them had even passed from this life, leaving her with all the full range of emotions that mark changes in one's life.

These days Emma seldom thought of *Lavender Blue*. It was as if she were two different people—the old her and the new. She had settled into life at *Arctic White* and now called it home. Grateful for Sven and Daria, she welcomed their friendship even as she defied Sven's advice to remain inside and take up womanly crafts.

She purchased snowshoes, for example, and used them to explore the land Hans Derrkstad had left to her. Always, she took Jake along, just to be safe. Together they found a myriad of interesting treasures—things like the den of some snowshoe hares, another that Sven later told her belonged to a bear, and the occasional encounter with moose.

On one particularly bright day, she enjoyed seeing an ermine scurry atop the snow, scampering across rocks and fallen limbs as it foraged for food. She had seen women with ermine coats in London, which made the sighting of the tiny weasel even more amazing. How many of these did it take to make a whole coat? Surely one made of something larger would be more practical!

She also reveled in the sighting of giant cat prints in the snow, watching patiently for days to see if the lynx that had made them returned. If it did, she never saw it. How could an animal so large be so stealthy and lithe?

At night she often heard the wolves howl. Their call was eerie and haunting. Once she thought she heard one near the cabin, and had tucked her fur blanket more tightly around her, but when she checked in the morning, there were no fresh tracks in the snow.

About once a week, she joined Sven, Daria, and sometimes a few others for dinner and board games. During one of these visits, Daria taught her tatting—a tedious and meticulous type of needlework that quickly bored her.

"I'll leave those finer tasks to you, Daria," she would say. "I can keep myself busy with my journal."

And Emma did so, maintaining an almost daily accounting of her life at *Arctic White,* which she carefully detailed with the use of a quill pen and handmade paper that the wife of one of the railroad executives had given her after one visit. And of course, there was her book of poems by Robert Service, which she read from every night before falling asleep, never seeming to tire of his work. Life at *Arctic White* had only deepened her respect for his writing. If only she could capture the essence of Alaska with the passion and devotion that he had.

And so Emma's first winter in Alaska passed with the exhilaration of solitude by choice and with the satisfaction of watching unimagined destiny unfold.

It was well into April when she noticed more moose than usual hanging around. Because of the hard winter, Rudy and Helen had postponed their wedding until June, having notified their friends some six weeks earlier.

The moose seemed to be hungry, foraging for food even among the remnants of Daria's last summer's garden. The light had come back, too, and although the northern lights still appeared, it was later each night and after the darkness had once again fallen.

Emma loved the return of the light and took full advantage of it by going out more to explore the land around her. By now Jake just showed up each morning, looking at her as if wondering what adventure this day would hold.

"You're bent on defying the woman's role, you are," Sven called one morning. "From the size of you, I'd never have thought."

"Now, Sven," she called back. "Do you see me wearing suffragette white? You do not." Causing Sven to chuckle and return to tending his dogs.

On this morning she had wandered out of sight of *Arctic White* in order to reach a pond where the first returning swans had set down from their migration on the slop ice that would soon become their summer home.

She was wearing snowshoes as the snow was not only still deep, but also grainy and sharp. She heard a low growl from Jake before feeling herself flying through the air—and that was the last she remembered. When she came to, she was inside a small cabin, with several quilts piled on top of her. Across the room sat a man sitting with his back to her, hovered over a table lit only by a seal oil candle.

She rubbed her eyes and sat up, but quickly lay back down when the pain in her chest took her breath.

CHAPTER THIRTY-SIX
WILDERNESS HERO

"So, you've decided to wake up," the man she knew as Nate Dryson said. "Careful now. That moose did some damage to your ribs."

Emma lay back down, clenching her teeth to ease through the pain as she did. Nate didn't seem drunk, which was a relief. But why was she here and why did she feel so terrible?

"If I got too close to your cabin and angered you . . ." she began.

Nate stood and came towards her, bending to fluff her pillow and tidy her blanket.

"Twas a moose," he said.

Emma furrowed her brow.

"A moose?"

"I heard you scream and when I ran out, you were on the ground—unconscious. Jake was fending off the moose. Then the moose kicked him and I didn't see him move . . ."

"No!" Emma cried.

"He's not dead," Nate answered. "After I fired off a couple of shots, the moose ran off, but the commotion also brought Sven and when he saw Jake on the ground . . .

"At first he blamed me. Thought I shot his dog. I told him, no, that a moose had kicked you and Jake had kept it at bay after that until it got him. I told him I shot at the moose, but missed. It was enough to run it off though.

"About then Jake whimpered and I helped hold him so Sven could check him out. His legs and head were okay, but there was a swollen area on his flank, so Sven picked him up and headed for the tracks.

"It seems like a miracle that all this happened right before the two-thirty Saturday train was due. Anyway, Sven got the train and took Jake into Skagway. He said he was going to ask Doc Johnson to check him out. Doc's good about that —checking the animals along with his human patients. Sure hope the dog's okay. Saved your life for sure. Good dog. Said he'd bring doc back to check you—probably tomorrow—worried you couldn't make the trip . . ."

Emma closed her eyes. The pain was bad. Every time she took a breath, she felt like coughing, but she wouldn't let herself for fear she would pass out from the pain.

"Here, take this," Nate said, pouring liquid from a bottle that said *Elixir of Coca—for coughs and pain*. "Should help with the pain and I'll make you a comfrey poultice for your ribs. It'll speed up the mending of your bones."

Emma did as instructed, feeling the combined sense of euphoria and pain relief brought on by the elixir.

Over the next few hours, she drifted in and out of wakefulness, aware of the slow movement of Nate around the room, and her consciousness interspersed with visions of flying moose hooves and searing pain.

When she awoke, the smell of soup filled the air.

"Had a coupla cranes stored in the cache," Nate said. "Some good eating for ya."

Emma took a sip of the hot broth and nodded that it was indeed good, setting the bowl down for a moment while Nate adjusted her pillow and blankets, sitting her up a bit to make sure she didn't choke.

The process with the coca elixir and fitful sleep repeated through the rest of the day and night as Nate stood watch—even assisting Emma with the chamber pot that allowed her to relieve herself inside, without having to try to use the outhouse.

By the next afternoon, the comfrey poultice was affording her some relief and she was awake and sitting up when Sven returned with Doc Johnson.

"You're in good hands with Daniel," Doc told her. "Nothing I can add to this regimen at all except to tell you that your lungs sound good, the bruising will heal in time, and the ribs will knit back together eventually. Until then, you should splint your chest with this band and keep letting Daniel apply the poultice."

Emma sank back into her pillows as Doc Johnson spoke with Sven and Daniel. She could hear them speaking but was only able to catch snippets of their conversation.

"... so, fortunately, she won't need chest drainage. Besides, creating the right amount of suction would be next to impossible in these conditions."

"Is there anything else I can do?"

"If the situation should worsen, don't hesitate . . ."

"Thank you for coming up, Doc Johnson . . ."

When the doctor had finally left, Emma allowed herself to fall asleep. She had faced adversity before and knew she could face this one. The fact that she was doing so in the company of a man who had once tried to shoot her was almost as big a shock as it had been to learn about the relationship between Rudy and Helen.

Arctic life had indeed been interesting so far. No wonder Robert Service had been able to write with such colorful abandon.

By the time she woke again it was morning.

"I made you some oatmeal," Daniel said. "And Daria's bringing some moose for dinner."

Emma nodded her appreciation, before coughing, grabbing her chest to splint the pain, and lying back down.

"We've all kind of decided you're best off staying right here for now," Daniel continued. "You'll be safe here and we'll all be watching over you."

Emma looked at him. For the first time, she noticed his hazel eyes were clear and bright and he had the fresh smell of castile soap about him, and a clean-shaven face.

She watched as he busied himself about the cabin, putting things away, straightening books and papers, stacking dishes, and generally tidying up.

"I want you to know I stopped drinking," he suddenly blurted out. "And I don't intend to start again."

She continued to watch as he turned his back and busied himself, before turning to her again.

"It's because of you," he said. "I won't let you down."

CHAPTER THIRTY-SEVEN

EARLY SPRING

By the end of another week, Emma was doing well enough to return to *Arctic White*. Although she no longer needed the comfrey poultice, she still required assistance with her chores and with cooking, and still relied on the coca elixir at night. All in all, though, she was doing better than even she expected and her friends were right there to check on her at least three times a day.

Daniel had come by once, then no more—which she attributed to his probably going back to drinking. She said as much to Daria one day and was surprised at her friend's response.

"Not only is our Daniel no longer drinking, but he's stopped referring to himself as Nate and has started attending services with us when the minister comes up from Skagway."

At a loss for words, Emma could only nod.

"Not only is he reaching out more, he's begun sprucing up his cabin, starting with scrubbing all the old blood off the bear spikes around the windows and burning some of the trash he let accumulate in his yard," Daria said.

Spring had indeed come early to Alaska, and although frost still marked the nights, the days often reached balmy high forties.

Emma loved the smell of the fresh air and had even taken to leaving her bedroom window open at night, secure in knowing that the old iron wagon wheel Sven had nailed across the window was enough to keep even the most determined bear from coming inside.

Her lungs had all but healed, too, as had her ribs, although an occasional fit of coughing reminded her that the moose attack had taken its toll. Although she often heard pounding coming from the direction of Daniel's cabin, he still had not visited, and so one day she decided to take matters into her own hands and take him a fresh loaf of bread she had baked that morning.

Jake had also healed from his wounds and had once again begun showing up at her doorstep, so on this day, she took him along, as well as her bear rifle—just in case.

She saw Daniel before he saw her. He had put on a little weight. Not to the point of heaviness, but more along the lines of a beefiness that enhanced his tall frame. Only recently had Daria told her that his last name was Harding, and so she called out to him, so as not to startle him or worse.

"Mr. Harding. It's Emma Brownston."

When he didn't turn around, she tried again.

"I thought you might enjoy some fresh-baked bread. I made it this morning."

She watched him slowly step down from the ladder he had been using to reach the roofline of his cabin, where he was beginning to check and repair the chinking.

"Mrs. Brownston," he nodded, removing the tattered cap from his head.

"I've never repaid you," she said, "and certainly one loaf of bread is wholly inadequate considering all you have done to help me recover from the moose attack."

"No repayment is necessary, Mrs. Brownston," he replied.

"Please, call me Emma," she answered.

"It does smell mighty fine," he said, softening his tone a bit.

"It's whole grain with a little flaxseed for both health and flavor," she replied, handing it to him.

"I'll be sure to enjoy," he answered.

"I know this may see somewhat forward, and possibly even unappreciated," she continued with a temerity that came as a surprise, even to herself.

"But I will be attending a wedding in Skagway in a few weeks, and I was wondering . . . I hope it does not seem too forward . . . I have been thinking that it would be to my liking if you were to agree to join me."

She watched Daniel's face flush as he turned away.

"I'm sorry," she sputtered. "Perhaps my invitation is unwanted, or perhaps you would find it tedious to accompany me for so long a trip."

He turned to face her, still saying nothing.

"It's just that I will be taking a cake, and some other things, and extra help—not to mention companionship at such a joyous occasion—would be more than appreciated. But if you—"

"Forgive my hesitation," he answered. "It is only so because I am humbled and honored by your request."

"Of course, in the matter of accommodations," she continued. "I have my own apartment there with an extra room should you need it."

Daniel's face flushed again.

"Of course," he replied. "It would be my honor to accompany you."

"Thank you," she said. "I'll supply you with the details soon."

Emma began to walk away before turning to say, "June ninth. The wedding is on June ninth."

Before Daniel could reply, she and Jake had disappeared over the knoll that separated their two properties.

CHAPTER THIRTY-EIGHT

RELIEF, OF SORTS . . .

When Emma returned from the weekly Saturday dinner with Sven and Daria, she found the following note nailed to her door:

MISS EMMA,

I FULLY INTEND TO KEEP MY PROMISE TO ACCOMPANY YOU TO THE WEDDING IN SKAGWAY ON JUNE 9TH, SO PLEASE DON'T BE ALARMED IF YOU DO NOT SEE ME UNTIL CLOSE TO THAT DATE. I HAVE DECIDED TO RETURN TO MY CLAIM AND SEE IF I CAN FIND A WAY TO OPEN IT AGAIN.

SINCERELY,

DANIEL HARDING

She hadn't yet told either of them about the invitation she had extended to their neighbor. She would—eventually—since they would all be traveling on the train to Skagway together. Maybe the fact that Daniel was gone until then would be for the best. It had been an impulsive move to invite him, and although he seemed genuinely pleased that she had, she had not yet found a way to explain to herself why she had taken such a step.

Besides, she had plenty to do with spring-cleaning of *Arctic White*, especially around the outside of the cabin, where mounds of frozen snow still made her walkway treacherous.

Sven had told her not to chip the ice as it would be too strenuous an undertaking for a lady, but Emma had already removed a good portion of it by the time Sven confronted her in the yard one day.

"I've seen my share of stubborn out here in the wilds of this frontier," he began, "but I'll admit I've never seen the likes of one as stubborn as you—and a woman no less, I have to say!"

Emma hugged him, throwing him off guard as she so loved to do, all while secretly thanking him for looking out for her. Daria had married a good man and she felt fortunate to have them both as friends. As much as she tried to repay that, though, her efforts always seemed inadequate considering how much they had done for her.

"Well, I guess I'll go check on Dan'l's cabin," Sven said. "C'mon Jake."

By that evening, she knew Sven had been right about one thing. Ice chipping was hard on the shoulders. She rubbed some liniment on them before stoking the fire and pulling up a stool close by.

She had barely finished the entry into her journal when sleep overtook her and when she awoke in the morning she was lying on the settee with the fur coverlet thrown over herself.

The knock on the door startled her awake. Since she was already fully clothed, it only took a minute to see who was there.

"Rudy?"

"I hope you don't mind if I call unannounced," he said, "but I missed our visit last time and thought you might be willing to at least offer me a cup of tea."

A cup of tea was the least she could do and Emma prepared it readily for her friend.

"Did Helen accompany you?"

"No, she's tending the office. I'm here on a spring bear hunt, but so far no luck. So, I'll be heading back to Skagway on the afternoon train."

"Then I'll also prepare you lunch," she insisted, as she invited Rudy to sit near the fire while she prepared something nice for them.

"Helen is so pleased you have agreed to make our cake," he said.

"I only hope it meets her expectations," Emma replied.

"I know our relationship came as a surprise to you," Rudy continued. "But you should know that it also came as a surprise to me."

Emma watched him as he chuckled.

"Who woulda thought an old geezer such as myself . . ."

Emma took a few bites of her lunch before responding. Sensing that Rudy wanted her approval, she chose her words carefully.

"I've seen the love you share when I look at you together," she said. "I see peacefulness on your face that was not there before, and I see the same on hers. For both of you, my wish is for happiness as you live out your lives together. That is what I have to say on the matter, Mr. Munson, not that you asked."

Rudy Munson smiled.

"No, ask I did not," he laughed, "but wonderful you spoke up. Your acceptance means so much to me."

This time Emma looked down.

"Although I'm honored that my opinion matters, we both know I have no reason to feel superior to you or to your Helen. Know that it honors me that my thoughts matter and among the many friends I have found in Alaska, you and Helen will always be near the top of the list for me."

"I'll be sure to relay your thoughts to my dear Helen," Rudy said.

"Please do so for me," Emma answered.

Rudy pulled a pocket watch from his vest and stood suddenly.

"Time has escaped me! I have less than one hour to meet the train."

"May I accompany you?" Emma asked.

"No need, my dear friend," Rudy answered. "Sven is pulling up with the wagon right now."

"Then safe travels until I see you and Helen in June," Emma said as Rudy tipped his hat and walked out the door.

How lucky he and Helen were to have found each other. Perhaps love existed for some. For now, that would have to be enough to warm her heart. The fact that she had known no such passion herself was inconsequential at this point in her life. For now, she would revel in the happiness of her close friends.

CHAPTER THIRTY-NINE
LOVE IS IN THE AIR

As promised, Daniel returned several days before the wedding. The sense of relief that washed over Emma surprised her. The winter had indeed been long and just the sight of someone familiar somehow brought renewal.

Of course, Sven and Daria had been there for her and she for them, but still the days had been long, cold, and dark and it felt good to know that the hustle bustle of summer was starting to return.

Daniel looked tanned and healthy as he helped her carry her bags to the wagon that would take them down to the train. She would bake the cake in Skagway. It would be safer that way, but the cake dish was fragile, so she had bundled it into a parcel twice its size to protect it. She had also brought along extra clothes, including a fashionable dress she had purchased in England before leaving for Alaska.

Daniel carried extra bags as well, explaining with excitement that not only had he cleared a path to his claim, but he had found the remains of his friend and former partner, Nate Dryson, and given him a proper burial.

"It's as if the time waited to present itself," he said. "And a burden has been lifted from my soul."

Emma could see Chan Yang peering through her curtains as she and Daniel unlocked the door to her apartment. There was a time when Chan Yang would have been banging on the door and running any unauthorized visitor out with a broom, but on this day, there was no such action and the curtains soon fluttered shut.

"If you feel people might talk, I can certainly take a room to save you any embarrassment," Daniel said.

"Perhaps you are right, Mr. Harding," Emma replied. "I have come to take the trust and openness we at *Sven's Crossing* share somewhat for granted."

After assisting Emma with her bags and resting for a cup of tea, Daniel Harding left Emma Brownston's apartment and secured a room in a boarding house not far from the assay shop.

On the morning of the wedding, Sven, Daniel, and several men from town helped put up a huge tent behind the assay office, while Emma put the finishing touches on the cake, and Daria crafted the bridal bouquet.

"He's a changed man," Daria whispered when Daniel came in for some string.

Emma nodded and felt a blush creep up her cheeks.

"Why, Emma," Daria giggled, "Are you blushing in the presence of your escort to the wedding?"

"Pish posh, Daria. We both know I'm way past such girlish reactions. Why, I'm nearly forty now!"

Daria continued working with the flowers.

"Well, Emma, it does give a girl fanciful pleasure to imagine that romance is possible even well into one's matronly years."

"Hush, Daria," Emma said, "and tell me if you think I should add more flowers to this second layer of the wedding cake."

By late afternoon, preparations for the wedding had been finished and guests were beginning to assemble for the ceremony, which was to be held at seven.

She had already returned to her apartment and dressed for the occasion when a knock at the door told her Daniel had arrived to escort her across town.

She was taken aback when she saw him. Seldom since leaving England had she seen a man so nattily dressed, especially here in Alaska where men seldom shaved or engaged in the grooming habits of their more genteel counterparts in large cities across the world.

Daniel extended his arm and she took it, allowing him to escort her down the steps and up into the carriage that had been freshly scrubbed for the occasion.

"May I say how lovely you look this evening, Miss Emma," Daniel complimented her.

"Why thank you, Mr. Harding," she said, feeling the blush once again creep up her face.

By six forty-five all were seated inside the tent, and by seven the local pianist had begun playing the wedding march as all eyes turned to Helen, who was being escorted down the aisle by Sven.

CHAPTER FORTY

"YEA, THOUGH I WALK THROUGH THE VALLEY OF . . ."

A light rain began to fall as guests gathered under the canopy for dinner and dancing following the ceremony as Rudy and Helen mingled with their guests, appearing relaxed and comfortable among friends. A fiddle player kept things lively and as the evening wore on, the sounds of laughter and camaraderie filled the air.

Daniel had insisted on accompanying Emma across town for some extra cakes she had baked in case they would be needed. They were only a few yards from the assay office when a man known to most as Reverend Black and another man—a stranger—confronted him.

"Yer friend and the harlot married yet?" The stranger sneered.

Daniel slowed his pace slightly, tightening his grip around Emma's waist, as he kept moving.

"My friend asked if your friend and the streetwalker got married yet?" Reverend Black said.

"I'll thank you to let us pass," Daniel said evenly.

"Looks like we're going to have to see for ourselves, then. Pretty fancy happenings going on here. Kind of makes a soul wonder who's paying the bill," Reverend Black said squarely.

"I'm not sure that's your concern, Reverend. Now if you'll excuse us," Daniel said.

A small crowd had begun to gather around the stranger and Reverend Black, whose new church had recently been established near the edge of town.

"My fellow brothers and sisters of faith," Reverend Black began, stepping up onto some steps as he spoke. "The life of a thief is the life of Satan, and there is no bigger thief than the one who steals your gold under the guise of fair appraisal."

Several in the crowd nodded affirmatively as Reverend Black stepped up his rhetoric.

"If any of you can attest to the integrity of one who would take a prostitute as a wife, then let him leave now, for we the righteous will soon march in the name of the Lord to recover what has been taken from us and to issue justice to those overtaken by the evil powers of Satan."

"Are you saying Rudy cheated us? I always thought he was fair," one man said.

"So did I," said another. "But why would you, a man of God, proclaim an untruth?"

"I challenge you to think back to your personal exchanges with Assayer Munson and ask yourselves if a man of such humble employ would be able to afford the lavish event we see playing out before us. Then I ask you to consider his many recent absences and the substitution of his presence with the woman of questionable character he has taken as a wife. When you do, the answer will be clear. As your pastor, I declare we have a thief among us."

Reverend Black paused for emphasis, stopping to wipe his brow, which now dripped with the sweat of feverish righteousness.

Daniel stopped in his tracks. Whatever would lead someone, especially a self-proclaimed man of God, to speak in such a manner?

"Do you have proof?" he called to the preacher, as the crowd that had gathered fell into hushed silence.

"Are you challenging the word of a man of the Lord?" the preacher called back, before leaning over to whisper something to the stranger accompanying him.

"Lynch him," the stranger called to the crowd. "Lynch the assayer and his sinful partner, the woman of ill repute."

As voices from the crowd began to rumble, Reverend Black began praying out loud, "Yea, though I walk through the valley of . . ."

The crowd, chanting now with the preacher, turned towards Daniel, who suddenly pushed Emma away.

"Run! Run and hide! Go!"

Emma sprinted for the shadows, moving faster than even she knew was possible. As she ran, she heard a shot, and then another.

"He shot the preacher!" someone called. "Catch the murderer. Lynch him!"

Emma heard two more shots and then the sound of the sheriff speaking, calling loudly to the crowd.

"I'll shoot or arrest anyone who stands in the way of the law!" he bellowed.

"We want justice!" someone shouted, before more shots rang out and several men on horseback galloped down the street.

Frightened and confused, Emma hurried down the back alley towards her apartment, surprised to run into Chan Yang, who was also running through the dark.

"Hurry, Emma. We find safety. They know you with him."

"With who? What do you mean, they?"

"With Daniel. Preacher Black . . . been shot . . . dead . . . they say Daniel . . ."

Emma didn't argue, instead she pulled her coat tightly around herself, feverishly following Chan Yang through the back streets of Skagway towards her apartment.

"Stay inside," Chan Yang warned. "I go to my apartment. If they come, say nothing. Say you sleep the whole time. I do same."

Emma, her eyes wild with fear, nodded yes.

She locked her doors and drew the drapes, leaning her back against the door as if to reinforce its protection from outside dangers. Eventually she climbed into her bed and fell into fitful sleep. Sometime around 4 a.m. she awoke and decided to head back towards town to look for Daniel.

Wrapping herself in a dark coat and scarf, she crept through the back alleys across town. She would start with the jail. Someone there would know if Daniel had escaped or if perhaps he were inside.

When she reached the jail it was amazingly quiet, with an armed guard sitting on a stool outside the door, but no sign of the mob that had been there earlier.

"May I visit Mr. Harding?" she asked the guard, unsure if Daniel was even inside.

"Your business?" the guard said.

"I'm his fiancé," Emma lied.

"Fiancé, you say," the guard answered, squinting as he looked at her. "I'm going to have to search you first. If you allow that, then . . ."

Emma allowed the search, aware that the guard was being respectful of her stature as a lady of means as he looked for weapons on her person.

"You got fifteen minutes," he finally said, waving her inside. "And I'll be listening, so watch your words, ma'am."

The jail was dark with only one lantern lighting the desk outside the three cells that made up the inside. She found Daniel with his head in his hands in the cell to the left.

"Daniel. It's Emma," she said softly.

He eyed her with a look of surprise on his face.

"It's not safe for you here," he said.

"What happened?" she asked directly.

"I raised my pistol, I'm not denying that," Daniel said, "and I fired a single shot."

Emma gasped, raising a finger to her lips and pointed to the guard outside the door.

"I missed him, though, I'm sure of it," Daniel said, his voice now lowered. "I couldn't let him kill Rudy and Helen, so I tried to stop him with a warning shot."

"Then who?" Emma whispered.

"I don't know. Reverend Black was leading the others to the tent and I knew he and his vigilantes would kill Rudy and Helen if someone didn't stop him so I pulled my gun and fired, but as God is my witness, Mrs. Brownston, as much as he deserved what came to him, it was not my bullet that brought him down."

"I believe you, Daniel," Emma said.

"I'm not sure why you would," Daniel said, "what with my history and all."

"I believe you because I choose to believe you," she answered. "Yes, I choose to believe you, Mr. Harding."

Emma watched Daniel tighten his jaw, obviously trying to conceal his distress. It hurt to see such a strong man display even this momentary flash of emotion as she choked down the lump that had formed in her own throat.

"I don't know where the others are," Emma said.

"You have to find them and go with them. It's not safe for you here."

"I've no time for that now. I'll be wiring a lawyer friend in Whitehorse as soon as the telegraph office opens. He'll help you, I know it."

"But Whitehorse—it's not Alaska . . ." Daniel said.

"He'll know what to do," Emma declared. "I know he'll know what to do. I have to go now. Just know that I'll be here."

Daniel nodded and reached a hand through the jail bars to gently squeeze her wrist. Then he watched as she quietly walked through the door to the outside.

"Thank you, sheriff," she said as she moved past the guard. "Good night."

CHAPTER FORTY-ONE

RELIEF

Two long days later, a visitor arrived at Emma's door and told her that her friends were safe. It was the porter from the railroad—the same man who had told her the story about Daniel.

"They wanted me to warn you to stay cautious," he said, "And to tell you they are all safe and that Mr. and Mrs. Munson are staying in your cabin in *Sven's Crossing*."

"Please assure them all that I am safe and am relieved to hear this news," Emma said. "Tell them I'm working with a lawyer to free Mr. Harding and that I will remain vigilant, but also that I will remain here."

With that, the engineer left before the breaking morning sun brought more people into the streets and with them, increased risk of his being seen at Emma's apartment.

She had received a quick response from her lawyer friend in Whitehorse, who had advised that he had already contacted a lawyer in Fairbanks, who would be handling the murder charges pending against Daniel Harding. It would be about a week before he could reach Skagway, but he would arrive by carriage and would take a room in town until the trial was set and over.

For some reason, the furor over the wedding had been replaced with the persistent and fervent attempts of members of Reverend Black's congregation to see Daniel Harding burn in a hell of their making.

"The Lord giveth and the Lord taketh away . . ." a woman who claimed to be an angel of God cried into the crowd.

"An eye for an eye, a tooth for a tooth," members of the crowd chanted in return, their voices rising louder and louder with each repetition.

Emma tried to ignore their persistent chants and cries, but the group, empowered by the loss of their leader, continued to be a vanguard for retaliation against the loss of Reverend Black.

She had known, or at least met, many men of the cloth in her time, but never any with the hatred-spewing vehemence she was now seeing. She had thought the suffragettes overpowering and imposing, but their presence paled in comparison to the flock of Reverend Black, to the point that some in town had begun referring to them as hatemongers.

Since Emma never responded to them, eventually they ignored her, too, choosing instead to gather in common areas to promote their cause. She easily moved among them now, no longer afraid or intimidated.

When had she become so strong? The question was one she had asked herself on more than one occasion lately. Certainly she hadn't been this strong when she had first set foot in Skagway, nor later, when she had returned to Wembley.

She laughed as she remembered fearing the wrath of Chan Yang as if anything the old woman could do right now could impact her in a serious way. Chan Yang had been a changed woman since her husband's death, taking on a less visible presence in the community and softening—even if ever so slightly—her gruff persona. Even so, having experienced the unpredictability of the old woman's temperament, Emma gave the woman a wide berth. Thus, she was surprised to run into her landlord while visiting Daniel in jail one afternoon.

"Good afternoon," Emma said as she met Chan Yang at the door to the jail.

"Enough chatter," Chan Yang replied. "I know you want know why I here."

Emma felt her face flush. Strange, how the old woman could summon up conclusions at will.

"I don't believe I asked," Emma replied.

How was it that Chan Yang always tried to put her on the defensive?

"But perhaps you want to tell me."

"Not like you. Nothing serious, Mrs. Brownston," Chan Yang shot back.

Emma brushed past her and entered the office inside the jail.

"May I visit Mr. Harding?" she inquired.

As the deputy showed her to Daniel's cell, Emma looked back to see Chan Yang hurrying down the street towards home.

"Regular parade of ladies today," the deputy said, unlocking a door that led to the holding area.

She found Daniel sitting on his cot with his feet up on a bucket and eating homemade bread.

"Chan Yang?" she asked.

"Yup," Daniel answered. "She's been bringing me food for two weeks now."

Emma raised one eyebrow and then sat down, proceeding to tell Daniel about the Fairbanks lawyer and the fact that she would cover all fees associated with his assumption of Daniel's case.

"I've seldom enjoyed such generosity," Daniel said, raising his hand holding the still warm bread, and nodding appreciatively at Emma.

"I suppose I should leave you to your meal," Emma replied. "Perhaps some progress will have been made by the time I visit next."

A light drizzle began to fall as she walked back to her apartment. Undeterred by the weather, she packed one canvas bag with a few belongings, locked up the apartment, and headed out to flag the train for *Sven's Crossing*. By 2 p.m. she was onboard and by five she was stepping off near home.

"There's no one to meet you," the conductor said.

Emma smiled at his concern and showed him her pistol.

"I'll be fine," she said. "I'll see you again soon."

CHAPTER FORTY-TWO

REFLECTION

Rudy and Helen were both surprised and delighted to see Emma. They had been walking back from Sven's place when they met her at the door.

"I'm sorry I gave no notice," she began.

"Notice? Rudy laughed. "This is your home, Emma."

"We can never adequately express our gratitude," Helen added.

"I'm only here to replenish my clothing and gather a few things," Emma told them over dinner. "I need to return to Skagway to see to the trial, and . . ."

She stopped before finishing. Not having yet decided how to proceed, for now she would say nothing.

"It would be my pleasure if you chose to remain here indefinitely," she said. "At least until after the trial—where you'll both be safe."

The remainder of the week passed quickly as Emma busied herself with packing. She needed to be prepared. After all, who knew how long the trial would take?

On more than one occasion, Sven and Daria expressed their concern for her safety, but Emma assured them she was strong and safe in her apartment at Chan Yang's.

"It's not safe for Rudy and Helen," she insisted whenever the subject arose. "But I need to help Daniel by ensuring the lawyer is paid, and by keeping an eye on Chan Yang, who seems to have more than a passing interest in Mr. Harding."

"I've seen some strange things in my life," Daria laughed, "But none as strange as the images you just conjured up about our Daniel and Chan Yang."

Emma had to agree. Fresh bread, daily visits, home-cooked meals—they all seemed out of character for the woman whose largest display of warmth had been to grudgingly rent an apartment to Emma. But if there was one thing she had learned in life, it was that you never really knew what was inside most people's hearts and minds.

The day was warm, with clear skies vividly blue under the abundant sunshine of the summer solstice. Sven was working in the yard with his dogs when she walked up.

"Mind if I take Jake with me for a walk?" she asked. "And don't worry, I brought my pistol."

Sven nodded and smiled as she called the dog to her and took off down a path leading away from both cabins. The fireweed had not yet bloomed, but it was getting tall—tall enough to foretell that the coming winter would bring a lot of snow.

The lupine was blooming, though, as were the various wildflowers that she had so come to love. She walked along admiring the wild geranium, Sitka roses, and the flowering dogwood, jumping back once when Jake flushed a spruce hen from the brush.

It wasn't long before she reached the clearing that Sven had kept mowed around Daniel's cabin. She was taken aback at the boarded-up windows. Did Sven believe that Daniel would not be back? Did he, unlike herself, doubt his innocence?

She walked around the cabin, noticing the pile of partly chopped firewood that Daniel had been working on before the wedding. She almost tripped on a couple of pieces of mining equipment he had left on the ground, probably intending to store later.

For some reason, she pulled on the door to his shed, surprised when it opened. It was dark inside, lit only by the now boarded-up window, and smelling musty and dank. She could see piles of stacked wood, and lying on top of one of them, a pencil. Impulsively, she reached into her pocket and removed a small piece of paper she had stuffed inside. Placing it against the door frame, she wrote down her name and the full address to *Lavender Blue*, before placing the note underneath the pencil atop the woodpile. Quickly she retreated and shut the door. What had gotten into her?

On the walk back to *Arctic White,* Emma tried to push thoughts of Daniel out of her head. What did he care about *Lavender Blue*? She had seldom thought of it herself as of late. Except for the quarterly report from James Knox, she had divested herself of all involvement there, choosing instead to focus on life in Alaska. Still, maybe he would need the information someday, although it was anybody's guess as to when or why that would be. When she got back, she would give the same information to Sven and Rudy. Chan Yang already had it. She also made a mental note to give James Knox information on *Arctic White*. With as much gallivanting as had become her lifestyle, it was probably wise that all players in her life knew exactly where they might find her—usually.

CHAPTER FORTY-THREE
AND MORE REFLECTION

"We'll watch over *Arctic White* once Rudy and Helen leave and if you're not back yet," Sven told Emma on the way to the train flag stop. "Daniel's place—well, we'll do the same."

Emma nodded as the train screeched to a stop. She watched as Sven and the porter loaded her bags and then she climbed up the step to the passenger coach, turning to wave to Sven as she did.

She had found a good friend in Sven and another in his wife, Daria. The same could be said for Rudy and Helen, and perhaps even Chan Yang. Daniel, her neighbor, remained an enigma, though. She had seen him at his worst and she had also seen him at his best. It would be an interesting partnership if he and Chan Yang were to unite, but the thought of that alliance left her shaking her head and unable to grasp the potential of such a union.

She had picked up her mail from the table in the arctic entry of her cabin before leaving and only now had she found any inclination to read it. There was an official notice that the District of Alaska would be named a Territory of the United States in the coming year, a letter of acceptance from the attorney she had contracted with to free Daniel Harding, and a letter from England dated May of the current year, which she opened first.

James Knox, Esquire
Overseer
Lavender Blue
Wembley, England
May 1912
My Dearest Mrs. Brownston,
I greet you with the great affection born of years of loyal service to the estate you have so generously placed under my watch. Perhaps before I continue, you will note the raising of my status to Esquire—a prominence I humbly assumed upon gaining acceptance of our product from the crown.

As I have previously stated, Lavender Blue *remains the sole supplier of essential oils and lavender used in the creation of soaps and lotions for the Queen. In keeping with the salutation on all orders from Buckingham Palace, I have taken to presume that I am now deserving of the use of the term "Esquire" just as was your departed husband, Hershell. With that being said, I do hope you will forgive my temerity in adopting its use after my own most humble name as I continue to walk in the shadow of his legacy.*

Emma placed the letter in her lap as she thought of James Knox and how he had proven to be both trustworthy and conscientious. He had done himself a disservice by comparing himself to Hershell Brownston and she would point that fact out to him the next time she saw him. James Knox was no Hershell Brownston, nor would anyone who cared about him wish such a comparison upon him.

Her eyes fluttered shut as she pictured James Knox, his wife Miriam, their children, and *Lavender Blue.* The visions had lulled her into a peaceful sleep, for she did not awaken until she heard the brakes of the engine squeal as the train pulled into Skagway.

Daniel Harding's trial would begin the next day and she intended to be there to see firsthand how it all proceeded. She watched as Chan Yang scurried towards the jail with a cloth-covered basket, presumably for Daniel. When she unlocked the door to her apartment, the air felt dank and stale. Apparently, Chan Yang had been too busy to air the apartment, as was her usual custom, so she threw open the windows and left the door slightly ajar.

After putting her bags in her bedroom, she poured a cup of tea and continued to read the letter from James Knox. It went on for several pages, detailing the day-to- day business of *Lavender Blue Estates* before veering back to the more personal matters of his and Miriam's renovations of the house they had built, and recollections of the schooling and antics of the children.

> *In closing, may I on behalf of Miriam, myself, and the entire staff of* Lavender Blue *bid you adieu for now as I beg your indulgence in remembering with fondness, those who will forever be in your personal debt.*
> *Most Sincerely,*
> *James*

Emma curled up on the settee and closed her eyes, pulling the blanket she always kept there up over her. When she awoke, it was morning— early morning, perhaps 4 or 5 a.m. There was no sense returning to bed so she bathed, fixed herself some tea and toast, and prepared to leave for the courthouse as soon as the day's business hour should arrive.

She heard Chan Yang leave before she did and so when she walked across town, it was as she so often had, alone. She watched a young man unload newspapers from a carriage pulled up in front of the hotel, waiting until he left to buy a copy for herself.

SECOND ANNIVERSARY OF THE DARING ATTEMPT TO CROSS THE ARCTIC BY DR. CHARLES PERCIVAL, the headline read.

Emma had heard talk about the event upon arriving that first summer in Skagway, and of Dr. Percival's intent to drive his 1910 Detroit Abbott automobile across the wild tundra from Skagway to Nome. She had almost forgotten about all the excitement surrounding that adventure in her own excitement about arriving in Alaska. Amazingly, the renowned Dr. Percival had made it forty miles before the motorcar had broken down, forcing him to abandon his quest.

When she reached the courthouse, she took a seat on the bench that made up the back row, where she waited with the others for the trial to begin, wondering exactly how long the longest day of 1912 was actually going to feel.

Meanwhile, perhaps revisiting the exploits of Dr. Percival would distract her.

CHAPTER FORTY-FOUR
THE JURY IS IN

The trial ended after four days with a jury concluding that although Daniel Harding had indeed pulled his gun, the bullet that had killed the Reverend had not only come from a different direction, but was of a caliber different from Daniel's own firearm.

Emma watched as handcuffs were removed from the man she had once feared, but whom she now called friend. Daniel Harding was a free man.

"Chan Yang so relieved," Emma heard the familiar voice. "Time to celebrate!"

She saw Chan Yang rush toward Daniel, who was being led by the sheriff to a freshly saddled horse.

By the time she reached Daniel, all she heard was the sheriff's last words, "It's best you move on, Daniel. There's a lot of folks here who still think you were involved."

She watched as Daniel nodded and accepted the return of his personal belongings, which the sheriff handed up to him once he had mounted the horse.

"Mr. Harding—Daniel," Emma called, watching as Daniel turned in his saddle to face her. "Perhaps you will give me a ride back to my apartment."

Silently, Daniel Harding reached down and assisted Emma onto the back of his horse. The two had only gone around the corner from the sheriff's office when Emma suddenly jumped down, prompting Daniel to rein in his horse and do the same.

"Please excuse my boldness," she began. "But I did want a moment of your time, Mr. Harding."

Daniel Harding's lip curled upward ever so slightly on one side as he listened. For a woman so pale and so small, Emma Brownston had a temerity that would drive most men to distraction.

"It appears that you suddenly have the need to leave town, and as I have already purchased a ticket on tonight's steamship south, perhaps you will consider serving as my escort," she said.

Daniel Harding could not disguise the look of surprise on his face as he stared down at the woman who seemed to have wormed her way into his life.

"To be clear," Emma added, "I suggest this only in the most platonic of sentiments, of course."

Daniel Harding removed his hat and then placed it back on his head before speaking.

"And to just what location is it that your steamship is bound?"

"Seattle," Emma replied, "and then travel by rail to New York, at which time I will board another steamship for Britain."

Daniel Harding said nothing, instead moving back to his horse to adjust the saddle.

"I do assume that you have the fortitude to withstand an extended period in my company," Emma continued. "And surely a man who has spent the majority of his adult life successfully mining gold has the means."

"Now why do you suppose that I don't have my own destination in mind, as well as concern for my cabin and my mine?" Daniel Harding said.

"Both Sven Bjorstad and Rudolph Munson have pledged to watch over both our properties until our return," Emma said.

"You've actually discussed this—plan—with them?" Daniel said.

"Only in terms of your possible sentencing to jail," she replied.

Daniel squinted, then climbed back onto his horse, shifting uncomfortably in the saddle.

"Perhaps my suggestion is unrealistic," Emma said. "Perhaps I overstepped in thinking you might be looking for a temporary escape from all this. For that I apologize. What could I have been thinking in failing to consider that you might be more than content to curl up with your bottle of spirits back in your cabin for the coming winter?"

Daniel's eyes flashed a hint of anger at her words.

"If," he said with measured speech, "If I were inclined to return to my days of imbibing spirits, I would already be inside that saloon across the street instead of standing here listening to the most forward woman I have ever had the—the misfortune—to encounter. And further, my departure would have been accomplished with such haste, that in the wake of my exit your own comely mane would have been blown straight out of that stylish little bun you wear so well."

"Tonight's sailing is at 8 p.m.," Emma continued. "I will be first in line to begin boarding one hour prior to departure, followed by any others who choose to sail south on the last steamship of the season."

Emma walked away, leaving Daniel Harding no opportunity to respond. When she reached her apartment, Chan Yang was pacing nervously outside.

"Where Daniel? I plan party for tonight. He need bath and clean clothes."

"I'm sorry, Chan Yang, but Mr. Harding ever so briefly informed both me and anyone else within earshot that he had been asked to leave Skagway and would be gone long before the first stars appeared in this night's sky."

"And I should also mention, Chan Yang, that I will be leaving for the winter on the steamship tonight. Should anyone inquire as to my whereabouts, please inform them that I plan to return in the spring."

CHAPTER FORTY-FIVE
STREET JUSTICE

Emma dragged her bag behind her, frustrated that she had packed it so full that she couldn't lift it off the ground. Shouldn't there be a carriage for hire somewhere along this main road through Skagway that could give her a ride to the steamship terminal? She was breathing hard by the time she reached the hotel and much relieved to see a carriage for hire waiting there.

A crowd of people had begun to gather around the hotel entrance. As she got closer, she could hear voices rising and feel a sense of unrest, even anger.

"Scot-free!" she heard one man call. "Might as well hang the judge and the jury who set a murderer free."

What was going on, anyway? She handed the carriage driver his fee, plus a little extra for hoisting her heavy bag, as he informed her that he would take her to the docks just as soon as he watered his horse and checked the harnessing for safety.

"Frontier justice should prevail," another called out. "An eye for an eye . . . just like the good book says."

Emma sat within the relative safety of the carriage, willing the driver to hurry as he and another man loaded her bag and proceeded to tend to the horse. Within the time she had been there, the crowd had doubled in size and had become louder with each passing minute.

Was that Chan Yang coming down the street? Why in the world would she be out on a night like this? Emma sat back, hoping they would soon start the drive to the docks before the growing crowd caused any disruption or delay.

She watched Chan Yang move toward the crowd, laughing at first as she invited them to party in honor of the acquittal of Daniel Harding, but slowly beginning to retreat as the crowd began moving her way.

"What wrong? Mr. Harding innocent. He free. What is problem?"

Finally, the driver climbed onto the carriage and began to jockey the horse into a slow trot. Emma told herself that if Daniel Harding had any reservations about leaving Skagway, the sight of this crowd would dispel any hesitation he might feel. She looked back again in time to hear Chan Yang call out to the crowd, this time with a note of anxiousness and possibly fear in her voice.

"Man called Daniel Harding innocent," she heard Chan Yang cry out. "We should celebrate. Throw party."

"Shut up, woman" someone yelled. "Go home and run your laundry."

"Chan Yang no shut up," Emma heard her say. "Mr. Harding innocent. Not murderer. You judge wrong. Stop now."

"And how do you know so much about Mr. Harding," a man with a scraggly beard and mostly missing teeth sneered, sticking his face within an inch of Chan Yang's. "I just know," Chan Yang answered.

"Maybe you know more than you're saying," someone else said. "Or maybe you're just as much a murderer as he is just for saying he didn't do it."

Suddenly Emma leaned out from the carriage and called.

"Chan Yang!"

But if Chan Yang heard her she couldn't be sure, because the woman suddenly turned and began running back toward her laundry with several members of the crowd in hot pursuit. Suddenly, someone lit a torch and threw it on the roof, where it rolled down to the roof dip between the laundry and Emma's apartment before setting the roof on fire. The action was followed by others throwing similar torches, until Yang Laundry was completely up in flames.

"You stop!" Chan Yang wailed. "You wrong. Daniel Harding no criminal."

And then in a voice that would haunt Emma forever, Chan Yang screamed, "Okay! I kill Reverend Black. I use my gun. You happy now? He devil man . . ."

The rest of her words would not be heard as the laundry fell down in flames around her just as she reached the front door.

"Chan Yang!" Emma screamed, before urging the driver to take her to the docks as fast as his horse could run.

After waiting for the driver to unload her bag, Emma dragged it into the shadows where she stood for what seemed like an interminable time until one of the workers on the ship walked by. Although the steamship was not scheduled to leave for two more hours, Emma convinced him that she was faint from fatigue and after ship authorities were consulted, she was guided to her stateroom early.

Her pleas were not too far from the truth, for the sounds of Chan Yang's screams would not clear themselves from her head. Why hadn't she jumped from the carriage and tried to help her friend?

She knew the answer before the question even cleared her head. Nothing she could have done would have helped. Chan Yang had met her fate and had now joined her husband in the afterlife. But why had Chan Yang killed Reverend Black? She had often stated her disapproval of Helen and thus, Rudy. The answer would remain a mystery that died with her, for no matter how many ways Emma looked at the whole scenario, there was no explanation she could come up with that made any sense.

And what about Chan Yang's fascination with Daniel Harding? That, too, would remain a mystery, for as far as Emma knew, the two had no history together, nor did she sense he had in any way been attracted to her. As far as she could tell, Chan Yang's temporary befriending of Daniel Harding had been nothing more than an attempt to alleviate the guilt of letting a man stand trial for a murder he did not commit.

Still, for Chan Yang's life to have ended in such a way was a realization that Emma could not fathom any more than she could understand why Hans Derrkstad had taken his own life. Even as much as she knew the harsh realities of frontier life, the fact that she had lost two friends in such a short time living in Alaska was a reality she found difficult if not impossible to bear.

She began to shiver, with the shivers followed by tremors so hard that they shook her violently in her berth. For a moment she thought she would vomit, but that would have provided relief from the massive wave of nausea that wracked her body.

Somehow, she found the cough elixir in her bag and took two swallows, allowing its pungent smell to alter the taste in her mouth as it slid down her throat. She took another swallow for good measure and fell back onto her berth as the tremors began to subside.

Even though the blanket at the foot of her bed seemed miles away, she managed to pull it up over herself before falling into a deep, dreamless sleep. By the time she awoke, the ship had been under sail for most of the night and well into the next day.

She sat up, but was forced back down by the pain of a raging headache and a sense that if she dared move, she would vomit. Her mouth felt as dry as cotton, but the thought of drinking something only made the nausea worse. After a few minutes, she managed to right herself and make it to the common bathroom that was luckily around the corner from her stateroom. After relieving herself and returning to her stateroom, she locked her door and crawled back into her berth where she slept for the remainder of the day and subsequent night.

By the time the steamship pulled into Puget Sound, a week had passed and Emma had done little more than order food sent to the stateroom from which she stepped outside only to bathe and use the bathroom facilities.

Chapter Forty-Six

Solitude

Seattle was shrouded in fog when Emma made her way to the claim area to get her bag. She had planned to stay here for a couple of days before boarding the railway to New York, and she did just that, wandering through the many markets and shops that filled the town.

On one such day, she stumbled upon Chinatown and, unable to bear the sound of voices that reminded her of Chan Yang, changed her ticket so that she could leave on the morning train.

She had given little thought to Daniel Harding since witnessing the assault on Chan Yang, but if he had boarded the last steamship south for the summer, he had stayed as well hidden as she had, for she had caught nary a glimpse of him at all.

Amazingly, she had grown tired of her favorite author, Robert Service. Whether because of the loss of Chan Yang and Hans Derrkstad, or because of the real-life drama of Daniel Harding's trial, Alaska and the Arctic had lost their magic for now. What had once been a romantic, almost mystical yearning for all things Alaska, had been replaced with a fervent desire to focus on just about anything else.

During a long stop in Chicago, she purchased *Women of the Titanic Disaster*, by Sylvia Caldwell, immersing herself in the stories of those aboard the ship that had sunk after hitting an iceberg on its maiden voyage from England to New York, just four short months before. Even as the book terrified her due to her upcoming voyage from New York to

England, it distracted her and kept her from thinking about Skagway, Alaska, and her life at *Arctic White*.

While in New York, she visited one of the new theaters there and enjoyed a Broadway play, somewhat sad that she would not be there to see *Within the Law* scheduled to open at the Eltinge 42nd Street Theater on September 12, only two days after her scheduled departure for England. Oh, how wonderful it felt to enjoy the cultural amenities of civilization again

She had kept a wary eye out for suffragettes while in New York, especially after reading they had carried on a large march the prior May, but unlike during her last visit to the big city, she had no encounters with them, even though their fight for women's suffrage continued to escalate.

Unlike in Skagway, or any part of Alaska as far as she knew, in New York automobiles seemed to be everywhere. After a few days, the noise of them moving about the city's streets actually made her long for the solitude of Alaska once more, thus it came as no surprise that by the time she was comfortably aboard the ship bound for England, she was once again enjoying the works of Robert Service.

As she watched the Statue of Liberty fade from sight, Emma let her mind drift to thoughts of Skagway and Alaska once again. It was as though she had never really been there, even though she had visited twice and become fully immersed in life there. As long as she lived, she would never forget the people she had met there, Hans, Lars, Sven, Daria, Rudy, Chan and Yun Yang . . . the list went on and on. Did those who remained feel the hurt and betrayal about her Chan Yang had, once they realized she had left forever without bothering to say goodbye?

Thinking of Chan Yang made her shiver again and she tried to push thoughts of the woman's last moments on earth from her mind. It could just as easily have been her, she supposed. Not that she ever would have the ability to shoot somebody—but maybe that's how Chan Yang had felt, too.

How sad that Chan Yang had lost her husband. It must have been so lonely for her there in Skagway without him. What had made her snap? Made her shoot Reverend Black? As long as Emma lived, she would wonder about why Chan Yang had shot the preacher over two people she openly disliked.

She tried to read some more Robert Service, but found herself unable to concentrate, so she walked the promenade before returning to her stateroom. In three days, she would be back in London and her life in Alaska would be no more than a memory. Memory—just the sound of it made her departure from Skagway seem so final. Had it been—final? She locked her stateroom door and slept, just so she wouldn't have to think.

CHAPTER FORTY-SEVEN
JAMES'S ABERDONIA LANDAU

Emma had not resisted James Knox's insistence on picking her up in London after wiring him that she would be arriving by steamship. To her amazement, after meeting her at the docks, he escorted her to the first automobile she had ever seen in England.

"My goodness, James!"

"She's almost new. It's an Aberdonia Landau. One of the first in Britain," James answered, running his hand over the shiny black coach before assisting her into the passenger compartment behind the engine, then taking his place in the driver's seat ahead of it.

Emma watched the London streets within the safe anonymity of the vehicle, enjoying the comfort of the fully enclosed touring coach with its lush upholstery and shaded glass windows.

Things had changed in London in the short time she had been away. Previously rarely seen laborers were now milling about the streets among the nattily dressed old guard that frequented the shopping district. Why were they not at work in mines and factories outside the core of London as usual and why did they seem so unhappy? The air of unrest brought by their presence was palpable.

On many corners, groups of suffragettes waved to passers-by as if wanting people to stop to hear their message. Although these thin women in white intrigued Emma, she had achieved her own independence without any kind of public display. Why were they so unhappy, restless, and in need of attention? They seemed to be everywhere she went lately, as if their herding together in groups empowered them. In her mind, it did not—but then, Emma Brownston had never been one to seek attention.

The sound of the Aberdonia rumbling down the cobbled streets of London drowned out most other sounds and it was not until James brought the coach to a stop outside London that she was able to talk with him.

"My, but we certainly moved along nicely in your new automobile," Emma said.

"I've had her on a straight-away at thirty-two kilometers," James boasted, "But generally our cruising speed is about twenty-five kilometers, depending on the road."

"I see," Emma said. "How very interesting."

"I apologize for hastening your departure from London," James Knox said. "I will assist you in returning should you desire, but the unrest is growing and I would not trust you there alone, especially if seen emerging from a luxury vehicle such as this."

James had alluded to the social uprising history would label as the Great Unrest, but until now, Emma had been unable to appreciate its impact on the streets of London.

"The rich are considered purveyors of obscene overindulgence by many now, and even oppressors of the masses," James said. "Thus, although I do still take the motor coach into London, I do so with the knowledge that I must remain vigilant while there, as well as refrain from boorish and obnoxious social distancing from those I meet about the city, lest I provoke their increasing tendency toward angry response."

"Well, my then, "Emma gasped. "Am I to understand that we must try to conceal our hard-won wealth?"

"That is precisely what I am saying, "James Knox replied. "Even within the confines of *Lavender Blue Estates*, all but our most trusted long-term employees can barely conceal their skepticism at our personal motives as employers."

"I see, "Emma repeated. "Then I will carry myself with humble caution and a wary eye as per your advice."

"You would be wise to follow my lead," James continued, "as so far, we have been fortunate to have been spared any major uprising at *Lavender Blue*."

Emma sat back in the motor coach as James drove the Aberdonia farther away from London. First Alaska and now Britain in social disarray. Whatever was happening in this world? If signs of this unrest were even presenting themselves at *Lavender Blue,* then perhaps James was right to try to shield and protect her.

CHAPTER FORTY-EIGHT
DISSENT

It was on a late September day when Emma felt the first tinges of unrest at *Lavender Blue*. The air, fresh from a fall rain, had lured her out into the fields, where only a hardy few of the lavender plants were still in bloom.

She had stooped to pick a stem, holding it beneath her nose to capture its waning essence, when a couple of long-term employees of the estate walked by. She watched them move past with heads lowered and voices muffled in conversation either ignoring her or not seeing her standing near the road as she awaited the usual custom of them greeting her first.

Later, she mentioned the occurrence to James Knox, who bowed his own head upon hearing the information, before summoning the two workers to his office, where Emma sat quietly in a chair off to the side.

"I will not tolerate disrespect for the owner of this estate," he said firmly, walking to stand next to Emma.

"Mrs. Brownston is the owner of this estate and as such is your employer. Further, she has held this position ever since the passing of Mr. Hershell Brownston, from whom you have held employ for far longer than I am able to recall."

James Knox stopped for a moment to let his words sink in.

"Should I find it necessary to conduct this conversation again," he continued, "The consequence will be the immediate termination of your employment with *Lavender Blue*. Thank you and Good Day."

Emma watched as the two chastised employees stood up and faced her.

"I meant no disrespect, ma'am," one of them said, "however, as a courtesy to you, I will reiterate that which I can only assume you already know—that being that many are rising up against the oppression wrought on us by the rich, such as yourself, who fatten their own coffers at our expense."

Emma sat in quiet disbelief. She, James Knox, and Hershell before her, had always been generous to a fault in the determination of wage values and working conditions for their employees.

She slowly stood, turning to face the two directly and not blinking as she spoke.

"Although Mr. Knox has full leadership responsibility as the purveyor of this estate, I can assure you that both our accounting firm and myself directly monitor such things as time worked, wages, privileges, and so forth.

"Furthermore, I need not remind especially the two of you that Mr. Knox upgraded employee accommodations within the past two years and has lobbied for and succeeded in achieving for you, a pay scale that is at least fifteen percent higher than on any other farm in Britain.

"Therefore, should either of you or any of your counterparts under the employ of *Lavender Blue* continue to feel oppressed enough to join the labor movement you are describing, then immediate arrangements will be made to allow you to acquire the necessary time on a permanent basis."

Emma did not wait to see their reaction, instead turning and walking over to James Knox, whose hand she shook firmly before exiting the office.

When she saw the same workers toiling in the field the next day, she smiled quietly and moved past them, not bothering to look as they both nodded and curtsied and said, "Ma'am."

CHAPTER FORTY-NINE

A KNOCK AT THE DOOR

Almost a fortnight later to the day, Emma answered a knock on her door to find James Knox standing there, his hat in his hand. The day was Saturday and the time around noon. She had been reading when the knock came, and appeared relaxed with her hair down and dressed in a casual frock.

"Forgive the disturbance, Miss Emma, but there is a gentleman caller at the gate who insists he knows you and assures me his presence will be welcome."

Emma furrowed her brow ever so slightly as James Knox continued.

"He presented this calling card and said it will be all you need to authorize his presence, which he assures me you will welcome without hesitation."

Emma took the card from James and held it to the light. It was printed on vanilla paper with a black script done in fine lettering and read:

DANIEL HARDING
MINER OF GOLD AND PLATINUM
SKAGWAY, DISTRICT OF ALASKA

"I shall have to amend my card soon," Daniel Harding said upon seeing Emma, "as the procurement of Alaska as a Territory of the United States of America is imminent."

"Daniel . . ." Emma said, barely able to disguise her astonishment.

She felt a flush creep up her face and a return of the giddiness that had washed over her before she left Alaska during her earlier conversations with the man she helped free from wrongful conviction in Skagway.

"Will you be in need of my services?" James Knox said discreetly.

"Thank you, James. No. Mr. Harding is indeed welcome here. I thank you for your vigilance in looking after me, but I will be fine now."

She watched as James Knox retreated down the stone walkway before inviting Daniel Harding inside.

"Would you care for tea?" she began.

"Tea is one of those English customs, I have learned, and so I will join you for some tea on this lovely Saturday afternoon," Daniel Harding answered.

The two spent the next several minutes exchanging pleasantries before Emma steered the conversation to more personal matters.

"After they killed Chan Yang, I swore I would never go back," she began. "Then I heard things that prompted me to warn you of dangers for yourself. When I boarded the steamship, I saw no evidence that you had followed, nor did I see any sign of you in Seattle or on the transcontinental trip by railcar to New York.

"Once I boarded the ship for Britain, I had already chosen to forget having met you, along with everyone else back in Alaska, as I vowed it was a place to which I would never return."

Daniel Harding turned his hat idly in his hands as he listened, watching Emma as she spoke, his own heart racing at the remembrance of the trial and his sudden exit from Skagway. He had been fortunate in catching the train to *Sven's Crossing*, and even more fortunate in having enough time to secure his homestead before catching it on its return run to Skagway before boarding the steamship that night.

She was as he remembered her, only more beautiful here in this setting so unfamiliar to him, but yet so fittingly her own. He sipped his tea as he studied her, noticing for the first time her naturally long eyelashes and the gentle curve of her lips.

As if sensing his gaze, Emma stood and left the room, returning with a plate of cookies that Miriam had brought earlier that morning.

Daniel Harding took what was offered to him as the two shared tea. Never before had he felt such contentment in the presence of another human. Not even with Nate, his mining partner, friend, and confidant had he felt this comfortable.

"I came to repay you" he said. "For the costs of the trial—and to thank you for taking the time to help me."

"I expect no repayment," Emma said. "I'm only grateful that your innocence was spared and your good name restored."

Daniel laughed.

"There are more than a few who would challenge both my good name and my innocence," he said, "but it matters to me that you believe in me and that, in part, is why I am here."

"In part?" Emma inquired, not missing the nuance in his words.

"Let me back up a bit," Daniel continued, "and assure you I was on the steamship on which we both departed Skagway that day, having returned by train from *Sven's Crossing* to see Chan Yang's laundry and home in flames. It was then I knew I must leave—that the angry mob was out of control and likely would come for me, too. When I saw no sign of you, I assumed you were protecting your privacy, which I took as a sign that we had permanently parted ways."

Emma leaned forward in her chair as he spoke, eager to hear more.

"When I didn't see you leave the ship in Seattle, I set about visiting some of my long-term friends and investors there, before boarding a train for the East Coast. Once in New York, I visited more contacts and spent some time looking for a market for my gold and did manage to attain the interest of an assayer there who supplies fine jewelers such as Tiffany and Company."

"I see," Emma said.

"It was when reaching into my jacket pocket one day that I found the note you had left in my woodshed—the note containing your address here in Wembley that I had kept in case I should ever need it. For some reason, upon reading it again, I was struck by the desire to find you, and so I purchased a ticket on a steamship to London, arriving there yesterday and finding my way here today.

"I must say, Mrs. Brownston, that upon seeing you, I do not regret my decision, as I find you looking rested and healthy here in this place of beauty that lends a whole new dimension to the person I first met so unceremoniously at *Sven's Crossing*."

CHAPTER FIFTY

GIDDY IN HIS PRESENCE

Daniel's visit left Emma feeling off balance. Of course, it had been wonderful to see an old friend, and of course, she was relieved he was free of the trial and the accusations of a murder he did not commit, but there was more.

For example, she had never really noticed how tall he was—at least six feet, and that his eyes were blue to balance the red hair that had begun to gray. His face was lined from years of working in the sun, but at the age of fifty, he stood tall and straight and carried himself well. Why, she was nearly forty herself and could only hope to look so good in another ten years!

It was nice he had found her, but hadn't she facilitated that by leaving the address for *Lavender Blue* in his woodshed? She found herself questioning her own emotions, wondering why she felt giddy in his presence and why she would even care about this man, who everyone said had such a tortuous past.

She had seen through that tough persona from day one. What was it that made her bother to look beneath the surface of this man? Certainly, she was glad that she had. Daniel had turned out to be a gentleman and a man of honor once he had decided to put down all his personal angst over the death of his mining partner and friend.

When he returned to her door a few days later, she felt happy. And on his third visit, when she opened her door to find him on bent knee, she readily said yes to his proposal of marriage despite her own fear that it was he who would find her disappointing.

She shared the news with James and Miriam Knox, and accompanied them, along with Daniel, to her lawyer in London, where details of their financial assets were defined and protected.

"Money's never mattered that much to me," he told her, even as she learned that he was twice as wealthy as she.

Still, they defined their terms and when the wedding took place on the first Saturday of November in the parlor of her own home at *Lavender Blue*, Daniel Harding placed a custom ring made by Tiffany and Company's premier jeweler and made from gold and platinum from his mine encircling a one-carat top quality Russian Alexandrite stone on Emma's finger as he pledged to love her for the rest of their lives.

"I do love you Emma Brownston," he pledged.

"And I, you," she replied.

And so began their new journey as Emma became Emma Brownston Harding, wife of Daniel Harding, Gold and Platinum Miner from Skagway, Alaska.

CHAPTER FIFTY-ONE

PARIS

Emma and Daniel left for France the next day, with James driving them to London in the Aberdonia, after which they traveled to Paris by railcar. It was as if the coming together of them as strangers had brought out the best in both of their personalities, with each expressing to the other that they had never known such happiness. Daniel Harding was indeed the man Emma had searched for her entire life and she the only woman to whom he had ever fully given his heart.

Together they explored the City of Love, dining at small, intimate restaurants, walking along the Seine, and like so many before them, touring the Louvre. They sent a note to Sven and Daria, laughing at the certain shock the news of their marriage would bring, while also knowing that their friends would share their joy.

Although initially leery, Sven had come to respect Daniel and it was a comfort to Daniel to know that Sven would watch over his homestead. When Emma and Daniel returned to *Lavender Blue* a month later, two letters from Alaska were waiting for them. The first was from Sven and Daria expressing their "complete and utter surprise" before wishing them well and assuring Daniel that his cabin was being well cared for. The second was from Rudy and Helen, who had decided to remain at *Arctic White* for the winter, but would be sure to vacate before the arrival of the first steamship in spring and the anticipated arrival of the new Mr. and Mrs. Harding.

"Rudy has decided to search for an apprentice for the assay office so that we can be free to build our own cabin in *Sven's Crossing*," Helen wrote.

"Should we plan to be there then, Mrs. Harding?" Daniel asked Emma over tea one morning.

Emma, a gentle smile of contentment on her face had nodded yes. But first, she and Daniel would spend the winter at *Lavender Blue.*

For one thing, even though James Knox was in full control, Emma wanted to teach Daniel about the farm. She had insisted that his name be added to the deed, just as he had added hers to his mining and business interests. They had professed in their vows that bound by the tenets of love, their partnership in all matters would be full. And so, to put it simply, on the day they wed, Emma became a mine owner and Daniel became a farmer.

Daniel spent a considerable amount of time walking about *Lavender Blue,* taking pains to remain unobtrusive, while not hesitating to ask questions of the workers when necessary.

"The cultivating and harvesting of lavender seems to be as much an art as it is a business," he told Emma after one long day in the fields.

Emma smiled at his words. Daniel was learning to love the farm as much as she did.

"We really must delay our departure until after the first bloom in early summer," he added. "It's a moment I choose not to miss."

Daniel also went over the books with Emma, James Knox, and their lawyer, but had no suggestions for change other than to inquire as to the logistics of shipping a small quantity of their product to Alaska, where he felt certain a ready market awaited it.

As the calendar turned to 1913, Daniel Harding found himself not only happily married, but also the proud coowner of a lavender farm, neither of which he would once ever have considered a possibility.

For her part, Emma remained as content as she could ever have imagined being. Surely, she had not been looking for love when she first met Daniel, and seldom had a less desirable character presented himself than had been the one she now shared her life with.

"It's like destiny brought us together—almost against our collective will," she said to her husband one afternoon as he sat cleaning his boots.

Daniel continued as she spoke, polishing the leather to a high luster while silently telling himself he had to agree. When he was finished, he went to her and held her and thanked her for being his wife.

He didn't see the tears of joy in her eyes as she nuzzled her head into his chest, but he did feel a love unlike any he had ever known, and for that he considered himself luckier than any man he had ever met.

CHAPTER FIFTY-TWO
RELUCTANT DEPARTURE

As winter rains and dreary days drove most Briton's inside, Emma and Daniel began to make plans for their return to Skagway. As usual, they would travel by steamship to New York, but instead of lingering there as they had done on the way to England, this time they would board the first rail express west, where they would depart from Seattle on another steamship north.

Having left most of their arctic gear and clothing at *Sven's Crossing*, they would travel more lightly this time as well, except for a few necessary personal items and the bundles of lavender sachets and soaps they were bringing for their friends in Alaska.

By March, signs of unrest had begun to resurface in the agricultural sectors of Europe, including at *Lavender Blue*. It had begun with the preparation of the fields and early planting readiness on the farm, when workers began reporting blocked supply chains and threats to blockade shipments if any crops were to actually be planted and harvested.

James Knox had been aware of the movement for some time, having often overheard bits and pieces of the grumbles of discontent. By the time Daniel and Emma became aware, the unrest had already erupted not only in the agricultural regions, but also in the shipping and transportation sectors of Britain.

Instead of the usual friendly greetings from the workers at *Lavender Blue*, James, Daniel, and even Emma were now being met with indifference and a palpable discomfort from even their longtime workers.

"Perhaps we should postpone our Alaska trip," Emma said to James Knox one day.

"Ma'am, with all due respect to you and to Mr. Harding, my wish is that you will continue to live your lives without worry or fear for the well-being of *Lavender Blue*."

And so, on a cloudy day in early June, with the lavender fields in full bloom, James Knox loaded Emma, Daniel, and their luggage into the Aberdonia and drove them to London where he waited at the steamship dock until their ship pulled away to begin its journey to the United States and Alaska.

Before leaving, Emma had extracted a promise from James that he would wire her if there were any need for her and Daniel to return to *Lavender Blue*. Although James Knox had reluctantly agreed, both Emma and Daniel knew it was unlikely that he would summon them except under the most extreme circumstances and that any such situation would require an immediate response on their part. As they departed England, it was with the subtle knowledge they could be forced to return to Britain at any time and with very little notice.

News of the strife in Britain and its spread across Europe had already reached America. Tensions about the status of the world stage seemed to lend a palpable aura of unrest everywhere Emma and Daniel stopped in New York City.

Unlike previous visits, the suffragettes, once relegated to dark alleys and back rooms of the city, were now front and center, waving their signs on public streets and in front of government buildings for all to see.

"They seem determined," Daniel whispered.

"Just nod politely," Emma cued him. "That way they will perceive support and not try to approach you."

Emma's plan worked well, and by the time the train had made its way across America to Seattle, the suffragettes, remembrances of the burgeoning Great Unrest, and all thoughts but Alaska had fallen into the far reaches of both Daniel and Emma's minds.

As they departed Seattle on the steamship *Cordova*, Emma once again began reading the works of Robert Service, with her husband, Daniel having become a late but fervent new fan of his wife's favorite poet.

CHAPTER FIFTY-THREE

HOME

The railyard in Skagway was crowded and filled with puddles and mud from recent heavy rains. By the time they had trekked to the station and boarded the next train for *Sven's Crossing*, Emma's dainty city boots were covered in mud and Daniel sported an equally thick ring of wet muck around the cuffs of his pants.

They had originally planned to stay one night in Skagway, but after looking at the uncleared, charred remains of what had once been Chan Yang's laundry, they changed plans and forged ahead. Rest would come later.

Even Robert Service's poems were not enough to shake the pall that had fallen over Emma's mood at the sight of Chan Yang's old home and business, and as the train pulled away from the station, she leaned her head against Daniel's shoulder and closed her eyes.

The rhythmic clickety-clack of the train lulled her into such a deep sleep that she jumped up in confusion when Daniel touched her arm to wake her hours later.

"We're almost home, Emma," he told her. "We'll have to walk to *Arctic White* since Sven's not expecting us until tomorrow."

The walk in the clean air was refreshing. Already wildflowers were blooming along the trail to *Sven's Crossing* as the calendar approached Summer Solstice and the peak of Alaska's summer season.

Daria was just coming out the front door of *Arctic White* when she spotted them. She leaned a broom against the door jamb and quickly removed her apron as she ran to greet them.

"Oh, my! Emma! Daniel!" she gasped. "And you're married!"

Daria ran to them, hugging them both simultaneously as she called for Sven, who moving briskly, came from the side of the house where he had been working in the yard.

"Well, if my eyes ever laid focus on a finer sight, I'd have to say I'd be lying," he laughed.

Sven squinted as he looked at Daniel, taking in the full spectrum of the last man on earth he expected would be married to a woman as fine as Emma Brownston. Something about Daniel had changed. Gone were the angst and the turmoil that had lined his face for years, and gone were the distant stare and the hostile edge that had kept him isolated from even the few residents of *Sven's Crossing*. In their place was a gentleness and a softness that seemed to breach even the tough exterior Daniel had shown the world for years.

Sven extended his hand, pulling Daniel toward him in a warm embrace.

"You've come a long way, my friend," he said. "Here, let me take these bags to your cabin for you."

"What about Helen and Rudy?" Emma asked, noting that *Arctic White* was empty and recently cleaned. "Where are they staying now?"

"That's a surprise I had hoped to save for later," Sven said, as Daria stood smiling, "but as long as it's such a fine summer's day, let's climb into the wagon and I'll show you."

Neither Emma nor Daniel was prepared for the sight that greeted them when Sven pulled the wagon over a rise that gave them full view of one of the most beautiful valleys in *Sven's Crossing*.

A recently built small cabin stood about midway across the first meadow, surrounded by neatly cared-for gardens of both flowers and vegetables. But the biggest surprise was the much larger building directly to the right of the homestead. It, too, was new, longer than it was wide, and made of logs. Above the double entry doors was a steeple, and upon the steeple a simple wooden cross.

"Someone has built a house of worship?" Daniel said with surprise.

"Not only someone, but someone you both know," Daria laughed.

At that moment, both Rudy and Helen came running towards the wagon. Emma had never seen Rudy look so relaxed, and Helen was almost unrecognizable with her thin frame and long, flowing, naturally brown hair. As they reached the wagon, Helen quickly tied her hair up into a bun before reaching out to greet both Emma and Daniel.

"This . . . this is yours?" Emma asked.

"It is indeed," Rudy answered. "We have started a mission here in *Sven's Crossing.*"

Emma could barely contain her surprise as she watched Rudy and Helen beam with pride. Suddenly, two young children began running towards them—one boy and one girl.

"Meet our children," Helen said, wrapping her arms around the dark-skinned youngsters. "They're orphans from Huslia," she said, "and the adoption will be final next month."

"We hope to take in several more," Rudy added, "as we embark on our mission to serve the Lord."

Never had Emma seen such contentment as that radiating from both Rudy and Helen, and the sight of it touched her deeply.

"You both look wonderful," Emma told them. "Just wonderful."

CHAPTER FIFTY-FOUR

FRIENDS

How could so much have changed in the short time Emma had been gone? Yet hadn't she changed, too? Never in her wildest dreams had she imagined finding love again, not only love, but love with a man like Daniel Harding.

Her husband had proved himself to be not only rugged and pioneering, but also a man who possessed all the characteristics of a fine gentleman. He was handsome, too, and knew how to dress in a natty, yet unassuming manner that commanded respect wherever he went.

He was self-made, wealthy beyond herself, and he was educated to a level she had only recently learned to appreciate. And Daniel Harding was as unpretentious as anyone she had ever known, which made it somewhat amusing to watch others, bent on displaying their superior intelligence, squirm with surprise when he unassumedly upstaged them with his knowledge and experience on a broad range of subjects.

Life, indeed, had come full circle for Emma Brownston Harding. She pondered that reality as she walked across the meadow a few days later, stopping briefly at Daniel's old homestead, which was now occupied only occasionally when friends of railroad officials were passing through.

When Daniel got back from the mine that evening, they would enjoy a late dinner and probably turn in early. She finished the rest of the trek to Rudy and Helen's place, where she found Helen pulling weeds in the garden with her two adopted children running basketsful of the pesky intruders out to a ridge, where they dumped them over the side.

"Emma! How wonderful to see you," Helen called. "Children, go play now while I visit."

"The country life suits you," Emma said, laughing.

"Indeed, it does," Helen replied, leaving a smudge as she wiped her hand across her forehead. "It must be ninety-five today. Shall we go inside for some iced tea?"

Emma sat at the kitchen table as Helen worked. The home was comfortably messy, lending a relaxed atmosphere to all who entered.

"I suppose I could have dusted," Helen said, "but there would soon be more, so—well, perhaps tomorrow."

"A person would be hard pressed to eliminate dust and dirt in Alaska," Emma said.

Helen poured the tea and sat down.

"I've been hoping you would come by soon," Helen said, "So we could talk."

Emma sipped her tea as Helen relaxed. Marriage to Rudy had erased ten years from her face as well as the cavalier smirk that had been her former face to the world.

"Is there something weighing on you?" Emma said, tackling conversation head-on.

Was Helen trying to hide a blush as she lowered her eyes?

"I'm sorry, Helen, perhaps I'm being too forward," Emma quickly added.

"It's just that I worry," Helen began.

She paused to sip her tea. Her brow furrowed and some of the lines Emma remembered began to reappear on her face.

"We all worry," Emma said.

"I know. I don't mean that kind of worry, Emma. What I mean is that I worry that people in *Sven's Crossing* or the children, or others will learn of my past and judge me."

Emma lowered her eyes to think, breaking the silence only after she had carefully considered her words.

"Helen, you have become a dear friend—not only to me and to Daniel, but also to Sven and Daria and most everyone who passes this way. You are deeply loved by your husband and your children, and you are living a life that is blessed with abundance."

"Yes, I know these things, but . . ."

"There is no 'but,' Helen. There is just now, for each of us and for all of us. Embrace the present, dear friend. The rest is unimportant to your life."

"I'm not sure how or why you were sent to me, Emma . . ."

"Helen, please know that you were also sent to me and to each of your friends. Now let's plan something soon—perhaps a harvest party?"

Chapter Fifty-Five

DREAM?

One plus two
Plus three plus four
Makes for ten
Let's count some more

Four minus two
Makes two again
Add three for five
My smart young man!

Emma's eyes fluttered open as she tried to focus on her surroundings. The large, sparsely furnished room held several beds, each composed of white metal head and footboards and covered in white linens. They all seemed to be occupied and there were several nurses bustling about— their crisp linen dresses rustling as they moved.

Where was she?

She raised one arm to her brow, shocked to see her skin hanging loosely from her bones. Her lips felt parched and she took a drink of the clear water someone had left on the table next to her bed.

One plus two
Plus three plus four

Makes for ten
Let's count some more

Four minus two
Makes two again
Add three for five
My smart young man!

The singing was louder now—closer. Sitting up, she saw Daniel enter the room and remove his hat. Why was his hair all gray, and why were there wrinkles on his face?

"Daniel," she called, but her voice was raspy and weak—not the voice she remembered. "Daniel?"

Emma fell back into her pillow. The act of sitting had left her exhausted and she closed her eyes to try to stop the room from spinning.

"Emma, I'm here," Daniel said softly. "I only left to run a few errands."

She opened her eyes only briefly as she felt his hand cover hers, then she closed them again and began drifting into sleep. She couldn't remember ever having a dream this vivid and she told herself she didn't care if she ever did again.

When she awoke, it was dark. The strong smell of antiseptic pierced the air.

"Daniel," she called in a whisper, but there was no answer.

"Daniel!" she screamed.

Someone lit a kerosene lamp next to her bed and placed a hand on her forehead.

"There, there, Mrs. Harding," a woman's voice said. "Your husband will be back in the morning."

If there had been any color left in Emma's cheeks, it would have quickly drained as reality revealed itself. It hadn't been a dream. This place was real. She pinched her arm to see if she was alive and found that she was. Not only was she alive, but according to a calendar on the wall reading August 26, 1933, somehow at least twenty years had passed from her consciousness!

"I have to find Daniel," she cried, pushing back the blankets on her bed and trying to stand. "Daniel!"

"Give her a sedative," a male voice said.

"Yes, doctor," came a woman's reply.

Within minutes Emma fell into a drugged sleep that would keep her from wakefulness until morning.

CHAPTER FIFTY-SIX

NEW NORMAL

His head in his hands, Daniel sat next to his wife's hospital bed tired and despondent over this latest downturn in her health. It had begun with the fall during the 1913 harvest celebration in *Sven's Crossing* only weeks after they had returned from England, and had resulted in a lengthy hospitalization in Fairbanks. Doctors had told him that although her bones would heal, they could not predict if or when she would regain consciousness, as the blow to her head had been severe.

Despite the effects of tuberculosis on her bones, Emma had recovered and regained the ability to walk, at first slowly with a stooped gait and hesitant steps, but steadily progressing until only a barely detectable limp remained.

He had brought her home to *Arctic White*, hired a full-time therapist to help her regain strength, and patiently waited for her to recognize him again. By Christmas of 1913, he had been gifted with the sound of her calling his name and by the beginning of the new year, she had resumed carrying on normal conversations despite the fact that her memory of all events since the fall remained tenuous.

By summer, she had all but rejected further therapy, insisting she could walk just fine by herself, and convincing her husband that the therapist was no longer needed.

"I'm so grateful you think I need assistance in my day-to-day life," she had told him with her familiar laugh, "but do you really think I'm a doddering old lady who needs somebody to help her walk?"

As had become the norm, Daniel continued to remind her of the fall that had kept her hospitalized for months, to which she consistently responded with the same surprised look she had displayed since regaining consciousness while still in the hospital in Fairbanks.

"I must believe you if you say such a catastrophic injury happened to me," she would say, "but truly I feel normal."

As had also become the norm, Daniel continued to reassure her that she was fine, never complaining when the same conversation would repeat itself multiple times each day.

"There's a hospital in London that is doing a study on head injuries," Daniel had told Sven one afternoon, "and another in New York City."

"Perhaps if you give it more time?" Sven had replied.

After which Daniel had agreed that Emma's recovery might well take longer than he had hoped.

Daniel had also begun reading the poems of Robert Service to Emma out loud, which thrilled her to no end, but on each and every new day, she would again ask him why he hadn't read to her since before the harvest gathering.

By fall and through the next winter, Daniel had almost given up hope that Emma would ever be herself again and had begun traveling to the church built by Rudy and Helen to pray not only for her recovery, but for the patience to help her as best he could.

Although he had told her about the world war now raging across Europe, he found himself carrying the burden of concern for England and *Lavender Blue* alone, for even as he kept Emma apprised of current events, she was still unable to remember the details for more than the immediate moments of each new day.

Talk of life before the fall was their only mutual recollection, and so they conversed about those times as if the hours and days that were passing had not yet even occurred.

CHAPTER FIFTY-SEVEN
THE NEXT TWO YEARS

The permanent residents of *Sven's Crossing* had come to love Emma and Daniel, with each in their own way trying to help with Emma's recovery. Despite their concerted efforts, though, Emma's memory remained sharp only for events occurring prior to her fall, and although it frustrated everyone to have to keep repeating information, Emma's own loving personality made the effort more than worthwhile.

Helen had been particularly patient with Emma, often bringing her to her home, where the two of them would bake goods for each Sunday's congregation, and where looking after the children became a task Emma really seemed to enjoy.

During those days, Daniel had been free to go to his mine, where he had hired three new employees to keep the mine working and to keep the books in order. This had also enabled him to come and go at will, and to spend the majority of time with his wife, and over the next two years he had watched her steadily regain her memory to the point where only occasional lapses occurred.

Unlike at the time immediately following Emma's accident, Daniel had since decided to purposely keep news outside their immediate existence from reaching his wife, a decision made all the easier due to the remoteness of *Sven's Crossing*. Although they sometimes took the train into Skagway, he was diligent in making sure that she was spared the onslaught of headline news that had sprung from the onset of the First

World War that had begun raging in Europe in 1914 and continued even to that current time period.

For the most part, life in 1916 Skagway seemed untouched by world events, with sights such as the gatherings of suffragettes, which were a regular presence just about everywhere else, non-existent.

Although by then several states had already begun allowing some women to vote, with Alaska being among them, this progress had not only empowered women, but had given them added incentive to unite the rest of the United States and its territories, as well as modern European nations behind what was viewed as an inherent human right.

It was on one of those trips into Skagway where Emma had first become aware of the war after seeing a headline in a newspaper that someone had left on a shelf in the Mercantile, where she still went to buy supplies.

"Daniel, have you seen this? They say that war is raging in Europe."

The day that Daniel had long dreaded had arrived as he had finally had to reveal the truth to his wife.

"Yes, I have known about this for some two years and have spared no effort within my power in trying to shield you from this reality," he had told her.

"But, Daniel . . ." Emma had begun, with palpable sadness in her words.

"I will not apologize for trying to protect you," had been his firm reply.

CHAPTER FIFTY-EIGHT

THE HERE AND NOW

Sitting beside his wife in the hospital ward, Daniel put thoughts of the years since his wife's injury out of his mind as he shifted uncomfortably in his chair, while he waited for Emma to wake and have her breakfast. When the nurses brought her tray, they also brought a bowl of oatmeal for him.

"This is really good, Emma," Daniel said, gently waking his wife. "Will you join me for breakfast?"

Emma smiled and covered her husband's hand with her own before allowing the nurse to move her to a chair.

"We'll take you to the solarium as soon as you've had your bath," the nurse said.

Two hours later, Emma sat in a large hospital transport chair in the solarium that overlooked the Thames River.

"It is so comforting to be near the Thames," she said.

"Indeed, it was worth the long wait to find this place to treat your tuberculosis," Daniel said. "They have been using the most advanced treatment therapies in the world, Emma."

Emma nodded. The resurgence of her symptoms had come at a time when she had almost fully recovered from her memory loss and the effects of the fall. She now had full recollection of her life except for those two years immediately after her accident, but those recollections were blunted by the drugs administered under the prevailing logic that keeping her sedated was vital to controlling the symptoms of her disease.

"I'm so relieved you are here," she told Daniel. "The nights frighten me, then they drug me."

"It's only for your own comfort and safety, Emma," Daniel replied.

"Dear husband, my own comfort would best be served in my own bed at *Lavender Blue,*" she answered in a rare moment of alertness.

Daniel lowered his head and remained silent. If only he could find a way to take Emma home, but conditions at *Lavender Blue* were not suitable for a person with tuberculosis—a reality that he had explained to his wife several times.

When the letter from James Knox had arrived at *Arctic White* near the end of 1916, the news had been both distressing and sad. It had read, in part:

"The war continues to take a toll on life here at Lavender Blue. *As we are no longer able to ship and distribute our products due to both the war and the worker unrest preceding it, our crops have perished and our land lies fallow."*

A subsequent letter two years later had been equally disturbing. Particularly the part explaining the toll the war had taken on James Knox's personal life.

"I've lost two of my sons, one thirteen and the other twelve, in the battles. Although their mother had begged them not to join the British army, they had lied about their ages and done so as valiant defenders of the land. Miriam has never recovered from the loss, and I dare say that neither have I."

"But why not, Daniel?" Emma persisted, jolting him back to the present. "Surely we can afford to make whatever modifications are necessary."

Daniel patted Emma's hand before standing to pace the solarium. It was true that institutionalization at the sanatorium was taking its toll on his wife, just as was the chronic sedation being given to her by the doctors. Even now, as Emma pressed him for answers, a nurse watched vigilantly to assess the need to further sedate her lest any stress should cause her symptoms to recur.

"Emma," he began, "I have kept you apprised of some of the declines at *Lavender Blue*. The downturn that began with the Great Unrest has now been exacerbated by the mounting personal problems of our own trusted overseer."

"But James Knox would never let *Lavender Blue* fall into disrepair, "Emma said, suddenly sitting stiffly upright in her chair. "If there is anything I know, I do know that!"

Emma leaned back as a fit of coughing forced her against the chair back.

"He *is* still there, isn't he? With Miriam and the boys?"

Daniel felt a wrenching inside as he pulled up a chair beside Emma and began:

"Although I have been forthright in keeping you apprised of events at *Lavender Blue,* for the sake of your health, I have kept some details from you."

"Details?" Emma asked. "What details, husband? They *are* still there, aren't they? James, Miriam, and the boys?"

"I'm afraid I must interrupt, Mrs. Harding. Mr. Harding," a nurse said as she began to wheel Emma back inside. "The doctor has ordered another chest X-ray and they are waiting for Mrs. Harding in radiology. Then, I'm afraid, I am going to insist on administering another sedative so that she might rest."

"But can't it wait?" Emma asked.

"You must go, Emma," Danial scolded her. "We are fortunate to be at a sanatorium where such advanced technology is available and all this talk has clearly upset you. We can talk about James Knox and *Lavender Blue* later."

CHAPTER FIFTY-NINE

POST WAR ESTATE

Daniel paced the solarium as he waited for Emma to return. On behalf of the two of them, he had assumed full responsibility for *Lavender Blue* since her accident, and she had agreed to this even long after her memory had returned.

The truth was that James and Miriam Knox were still there, overseeing the estate as they had always done—a fact that Daniel in good conscience was regularly able to report to his wife. Despite the emotional devastation the death of their sons had wrought on each of them, James and Miriam had remained true to their commitment to *Lavender Blue,* which had allowed Emma and Daniel to remain in Alaska.

About every two years, Daniel had gone back to the estate to meet with James Knox and their lawyer, while Emma had remained in Alaska, where their friends could provide her with any assistance if needed.

The reverses at *Lavender Blue* brought first by the Great Unrest and later by Britain's Great Depression had indeed been catastrophic, resulting in the need to let most of the field workers go. Subsequently, their once luxurious housing now received only minimal maintenance and after all these years had begun to outwardly show the signs of this neglect. Issues like broken water lines and frayed wiring had made the residences uninhabitable.

James Knox had made a valiant effort to restore the fields, and production had slowly returned with the help of seasonal workers, but not to pre-war levels.

In spite of James's oft expressed desire to begin work on restoring worker housing, that particular undertaking had not materialized due in part to the fact that he now spent his nights, and sometimes parts of his days immersing himself in the numbing embrace of alcohol. This had created an even greater burden for his wife, Miriam, who had recently fled their home due to his drinking and was now living with her sister in London, which only served to worsen James Knox's already tenuous situation.

Although Daniel was not unsympathetic to James Knox's plight, he found himself increasingly impatient and disturbed with his overseer's decline. As much as he wanted to help, he knew from his own experience that James Knox could only begin to recover once he had faced his demons, thus Daniel had begun spending a good part of each day beginning to restore the estate himself now that Emma was being cared for at the sanatorium.

At some point, he was going to have to tell her about James, Miriam, and the boys. At some point, he was also going to have to tell her details about the war and the decline of her beloved *Lavender Blue*. It's just that he had hoped he could make more progress before he did, and that James Knox would somehow come to terms with the destructive effects of his drinking and be able to help him with the estate.

All of this had come to a head last week when Daniel had found James Knox slumped over alongside the main house and had confronted him.

"Get up, man! Can't you see you've become a common drunk? Can't you see you've driven your grieving wife away and let everything that ever mattered to you slide into chaos?"

James Knox had lifted his head slightly and gazed at Daniel through bleary eyes before lowering his head and closing his eyes again.

"I said get up, James!" Daniel had hissed. "Get up and behave like a man!"

It was only as Daniel walked away that he had heard sobs coming from the once stoic overseer who for years had served the estate with the highest distinction. Sobs and then cries of despondency.

Resisting the temptation to turn around, Daniel had kept walking, knowing full well that this low point was a necessary step if James Knox was ever going to begin to recover.

"Your wife will be returning in about five minutes," a nurse told Daniel, the reality of which made him stop thinking of James Knox and *Lavender Blue* for the time being.

Chapter Sixty
Room for Hope?

"Her chest X-ray is remarkably improved since the last study we did six months ago," the doctor told Daniel, showing him the particulars of the film.

For a young man probably not yet thirty, Dr. Smithson appeared confident and assured as he spoke.

"Emma will be so relieved at this news," Daniel said. "She has been steadily begging me to take her home."

"Interesting," Dr. Smithson replied.

"Interesting, doctor?" Daniel inquired.

"Interesting, as she has been saying the same thing to both me and the nurses," he answered.

"Is it possible she could be released soon?" Daniel said, trying to keep the excitement from his voice.

Dr. Smithson sat thoughtfully for a few minutes before answering.

"I can foresee such an inevitability," he said cautiously. "However, her night terrors are concerning, as is her continual insistence that she lives in Alaska—our concern being a possible inability to use oxygen efficiently due to damage to her lungs."

"She does," Daniel said, taking the doctor by surprise. "She does live in Alaska. I should clarify and say that she did, anyway, until our return to Britain about a year ago for the purpose of advanced treatment at this highly regarded institution."

"This information is new to me and I assume to members of our staff," Dr. Smithson stated. "This could shed new light on at least part of her nighttime confusion."

"Mrs. Harding tells me almost daily that she is afraid of the night and that she is drugged," Daniel said. "I, myself, have had difficulty processing some of her statements, but if in your own description of her nighttime confusion you have been sedating her, could this be part of an ongoing problem with facing the night, especially in addition to the milder sedatives she receives during the day if she becomes overly animated?"

"I will need to give this more thought as well as talk to the nurses," the doctor replied. "If, in fact, we no longer need to heavily sedate her for her own protection, then . . ."

"Excuse me, Dr. Smithson," a nurse interrupted. "But we have an emergency in the acute care ward."

Daniel watched as both the doctor and nurse rushed out of the room. A short time later, another nurse brought Emma back to the solarium, where she placed lunch on a tray in front of her chair.

"Your doctor is very optimistic, Emma," he told her. "You enjoy your lunch and perhaps a nap now. I have important errands to run this afternoon before I return to bid you goodnight."

Emma nodded and smiled as she watched her husband leave and move quickly past the nurses' station to an elevator that would take him to the ground floor two stories below. Clearly, no further conversation about James Knox and *Lavender Blue* would occur today.

As she looked out the window, she saw him wave before entering a waiting taxi, but by the time she raised her own hand to wave back, the taxi had already disappeared down the street.

CHAPTER SIXTY-ONE
HELP FOR A FRIEND

When Daniel arrived at the overseer's cottage at *Lavender Blue,* he waited for a few moments to gather his thoughts, after which several knocks brought a disheveled, but sober James Knox to the door.

"A cup of tea or coffee would be most welcome," Daniel began, "Before my driver returns to take us to visit Miriam in London."

"I'm not sure . . . I haven't . . ." James stammered.

"This is not about you!" Daniel thundered. "I'm taking you to the wife you have driven away with your drinking. I know you love her just as I know she loves you. Whatever you've done to drive her away, I'm hoping you can repair and convince her to come home."

James Knox stepped back, as if Daniel's words had jolted him out of his delirium.

"I'll prepare your tea," James Knox said somberly.

Daniel felt his stomach twist into a knot. He had been where James Knox was now, weakened, self-loathing, and afraid. If there was a way he could help this grieving couple, he would.

"Her sister is taking her in for a new therapy for depression," James Knox blurted. "It's the thought of that treatment that drove us apart. I told her I could not support allowing doctors to insert a probe into her brain to stop her from feeling. She accused me of not caring about her and of wanting her to remain sad and despondent when there is something new out there that could help her."

Daniel lowered his head. Was it any wonder James Knox had finally given up hope?

"God willing, we will reach her in time," Daniel said, "and if so blessed, we will bring her home to you, and to where we can spend whatever amount is necessary to relieve her depression in the least toxic way."

"But my fortunes are spent," James Knox said flatly.

"You have been a faithful overseer of this estate, to me, and to Mrs. Harding," Daniel said. "Although you have yourself fallen into despair, I have every hope that the deep love you hold for your Miriam will give you the strength and the determination to pull your life together. As for the money, I am wealthy beyond my wildest dreams of success and I will spend what is necessary. That is my decision since finding you in need of help."

"But I don't deserve . . ."

"Do not attempt to tell me how to best spend my own fortunes," Daniel shot back. "I ask only for your honest effort to recover your own dignity and nothing more. Once accomplished, together we will make *Lavender Blue* profitable again. Now, hurry. My driver will return shortly."

"I'll ready myself immediately," James Knox replied. "You are a true friend to my undeserving self and Mrs. Harding is truly fortunate she found you."

CHAPTER SIXTY-TWO

REFLECTIONS

Daniel reflected on his own life as he waited for James Knox to get ready. He had been where James was now. Perhaps he would still be there if for some reason he hadn't seen the futility of anesthetizing himself with alcohol. He had to credit Emma for helping him reach that epiphany. Without her firm hand, it was doubtful he would have allowed himself to care.

He consciously told himself not to be smug about his own success in overcoming the years of chaos his drinking had brought. It had not been easy to stop giving in to the call of the bottle, and he was wise enough to know that he was a very lucky man. It would be naïve to think it would be easy for James Knox. After all, wasn't there a certain amount of comfort in not having to face some of life's harshest moments?

He thought of Miriam. A quiet woman. He had never really gotten to know her, but one thing he did know of was her deep love for her husband, and his for her. Would that love be enough to pull James Knox out of his downward spiral? Was Miriam's own reserve, depleted by the loss of her two sons, recoverable and able to welcome her husband back into her heart?

No answers came to Daniel, and why would they? James Knox climbed into the taxi beside him and little was said between them as they made their way to London.

"Nothing matters more than she does," Daniel said simply once they had reached their destination.

Daniel watched as this once proud man walked slowly to the door of his sister-in-law's cottage, waited for a few moments, knocked, and was welcomed inside by a middle-aged woman wearing the drab clothing of the working class. For a moment, he stood outside the cab as if to will good fortune on James and Miriam Knox, then he climbed back inside and instructed the driver to take him to his flat across town.

He had promised Emma that he would see her before nightfall and he would be true to his word, but first he needed to think, and when he let himself into the small flat he had rented above a haberdashery, he went directly to the cabinet, removed one of the vintage cigars that he saved for those rare occasions when he smoked, cut it with the precision of an expert, and then lit it. Stepping out onto the small balcony that overlooked the Thames, he took several deep puffs and watched the plume form over the edges of the hand-rolled masterpiece he had purchased in New York.

There was something satisfying about partaking in this earthly pleasure that was best enjoyed alone. Certainly, Emma would not have tolerated such an indulgence in her presence. He thought of their years together, letting the emotion of his deep love and appreciation for her wash over him.

A light rain had begun to fall, forcing him back inside. If there was any way to bring her back to *Lavender Blue*, he would find it, and the sooner the better for both their sakes.

As for James and Miriam Knox, he and Emma would do whatever they could to make their path back to relative normalcy as smooth as possible, then, together, they would restore *Lavender Blue* to its former glory. Nothing else—not his mine, their estate in *Sven's Crossing*, or their Alaska life mattered as much right now. Thanks to Sven and Daria and Helen and Rudy, *Arctic White* would be waiting for them once their affairs in England had been completed.

CHAPTER SIXTY-THREE
REVEALING THE TRUE STORY

Emma was still awake when Daniel returned to the sanatorium around 9 p.m. He had already arranged to spend the night in a trial effort to see if Emma's fear of the night dissipated when she was not sedated.

After a nurse brought them some tea, they talked until well after midnight as Daniel filled her in on the details of James Knox and *Lavender Blue.*

"It's true that James Knox was steadfast in his desire to protect us from much of the news surrounding both the Great Unrest and the Great Slump," he told her, referring to England's Great Depression.

"His loyalty is above question," Emma replied.

"But beyond that, what I have kept from you is a detail so personal to their lives . . ." Daniel said.

Emma watched sadness creep across her husband's face as she tried to imagine what he was about to tell her. Gently, she placed one hand over his as she waited for him to continue.

Unlike most of the nights of recent memory, tonight she was calm and relaxed. While she waited for Daniel to collect his thoughts, she thought about years past and smiled when remembering the events of their first encounter. Never, back then, could she have predicted she would love this man more than life itself, let alone be married to him.

Suddenly, Daniel pulled his hand away from hers and straightened himself in his chair.

"There's really no way to tell you this except to tell you," he began.

Emma listened as Daniel told the story of how James and Miriam's two boys, both large beyond their years, had lied about their ages and secretly enlisted in the British army during the heat of World War I.

"By the time Miriam had found the note atop their unmade beds, the boys had already gone off to war."

"Oh, dear Lord . . ." Emma said.

"James told me he went after them, but in the confusion of the war, by the time their location was discovered, it was too late to retrieve them, as their unit was engaged in fierce combat along the front lines.

"Apparently, there was significant effort exerted by the commanding officer to remove them from the field, but in the chaos of battle, communications with higher priority prevailed, and the boys were felled on the battlefield alongside most of the rest of their company."

Tears welled in Emma's eyes as Daniel continued with the story James Knox had finally relayed to him years after his fateful loss.

"I only learned of all this on my last visit to *Lavender Blue,* made only a year before our own return to England. At the time, we were dealing with the decline in your own health, and I was immersed in my own battle to find a way to bring you to the care you desperately needed.

"Once we had finally returned and treatment for you had been secured, only then was I free to begin to address the issues at *Lavender Blue.*"

"How could James and Miriam have even concentrated on the estate?" Emma asked.

"What I learned is that despite a valiant effort to protect *Lavender Blue*— the massive reverses brought by the Depression and the war, the loss of staff, and the decrease in marketing options, along with their own devastating personal loss—what I learned was that the once strong, confident, and solid James Knox had begun using alcohol as a way to cope."

"Is it any wonder . . .?" Emma said.

"When I found him slumped beside the cottage a week ago, I knew I had to take action, so this morning I went to *Lavender Blue,* confronted him in as honest and firm a way as I could muster, and then convinced him to let me take him to Miriam, who, struggling with her own grief, had fled to her sister's home in London."

"And that is why you were gone today," Emma finished. "Oh, my dearest Daniel."

"You now know the whole truth, Emma, and I beg your forgiveness for keeping this secret from you, just as I know I would do so again if it meant protecting you from added worry."

Emma closed her eyes as she tried to digest this latest news. She felt Daniel's hand over hers and gently squeezed it. By the time she awoke, the morning sun was peeking through the blinds of her room as Daniel lay asleep beside her, still sitting in his chair, but with his head laid beside her knees.

A nurse bringing breakfast awakened him. After eating, Emma would tell Daniel of her restful sleep and assure him that her love for him had only grown deeper through the night.

CHAPTER SIXTY-FOUR

NEW NORMAL

Although Daniel went back to his flat for some real sleep after breakfast, he and Emma soon entered into a routine where he spent the nights at her bedside, eventually leading the nursing staff to bring a cot into the room to place next to her bed.

After a month or so on this schedule, and with no sign of Emma's nightmares or night terrors returning, Daniel met with Dr. Smithson, who agreed to discontinue the Chloral Hydrate and barbiturates that had previously been used to help Emma sleep.

"She has made remarkable progress," Dr. Smithson said during his rounds one morning. "In view of her improved x-rays and clear sensorium, I would like to begin increasing her activity—perhaps even encouraging interaction with some of the programs we have initiated here at the sanatorium."

"Do you believe it will be possible for her to come home one day?" Daniel asked.

"I would not be able to predict that at this time," Dr. Smithson answered. "I would not want to instill false hope, but we have also slowly eliminated the use of sedatives during the day as we continue to monitor the effects of increased wakefulness on her health."

Daniel nodded and refrained from further questioning. The fact that Emma had improved so much gave him hope, but he would not risk her health by insisting on her discharge from the facility. Instead, he would be patient and see how things went. Thus, after two months of spending each night with his wife, he gradually began leaving her alone for longer periods at night until eventually he was able to return to a normal schedule.

For her part, Emma worked diligently to increase her activity each day, until by October of 1933, she was spending much of her day walking the halls of the sanatorium or engaging in activities with other patients—such as a sewing club, and her favorite, a Christmas chorale.

Dr. Smithson's wife, Charmaine, was the director of both the children's educational activities and the children's and adults' choruses at the sanatorium. Although singing was difficult for many at the facility due to their lung disease, Charmaine and Dr. Smithson had begun a progressive program to encourage this activity as a means of not only decreasing the isolation brought by institutionalization, but also as a means of increasing deep breathing and lung capacity.

Their work had recently been spotlighted at Oxford University and other well-known universities around the world and they were in the early phase of refining their program with plans to launch similar programs in the United States beginning in about two years.

As the calendar turned over into 1934, Emma was fully immersed in life at the sanatorium and according to Dr. Smithson, was making record progress.

"It is too soon to trust that Mrs. Harding will fare well outside the controlled environment of this sanatorium," Dr. Smithson told Daniel one day, "But perhaps in another year we might well consider it. You know, current teaching advocates for institutionalization, but I'm not sure it's always best to assume that today's technology will serve as well into the future."

Daniel nodded. He felt assured his Emma was receiving the best and most progressive care of the day, and he owed more gratitude than he could ever repay, to the young doctor who had so diligently and skillfully directed his wife's care.

"Thank you, doctor," he said, shaking the young man's hand. "Without question, I trust your supervision of my wife's care and plan to initiate a generous endowment to this institution dedicated to funding further research into the devastating disease of tuberculosis."

CHAPTER SIXTY-FIVE

RENEWAL

James Knox had reached Miriam in time to stop the scheduled lobotomy and as he relayed the story to Daniel, she had, after several heated and emotional discussions with her husband, agreed to return to *Lavender Blue*.

From that day on, Daniel noticed a new determination in the way James Knox approached some of the many needed repairs around the estate. Miriam seemed somewhat better, too, and was often seen tidying up their home, Emma's home, and helping her husband with his chores.

As far as Daniel knew, James Knox never took another drink of alcohol after Miriam returned home and she ceased her endless crying at the loss of their sons, choosing instead to busy herself about the estate.

For his part, Daniel met regularly with their attorney to try to maintain a tight grasp on the assets surrounding the limited lavender production that would undergo its first harvest during the coming summer.

"This crop has already been consigned to the Queen's personal chandler, and if this agreement is as successful and the crop as productive as I hope, *Lavender Blue* should regain its reputation as the premier producer of lavender in England," James Knox told the attorney as Daniel listened.

The news brought the hint of a smile to Daniel's lips.

"None of this would be possible without the help of you and Miriam," he told James Knox.

"I have no words to describe my gratitude for your support and understanding, Mr. Harding," James Knox replied. "And have you been made aware that the Queen Mother has summoned Miriam to the palace to assist her staff in selecting the best products for her personal use?"

"Dearest husband, I was saving that surprise for later," Miriam said, walking in on the group.

She had taken to accompanying her husband on his travels now that they were alone with their personal lives, and although always invited to sit in on meetings with the attorney, usually she declined, instead preferring to visit the many nearby London shops.

"And a pleasant surprise it is!" Daniel said, standing.

He watched as a blush crept up Miriam's face, also catching a glimpse of the pride and adulation beaming from her husband's face.

"It seems my wife is somewhat of a creative genius," James Knox said. "How fortunate the Queen Mother has brought her out of the shadows of subservience to free her inner muse."

Watching an even deeper blush move up Miriam's face, Daniel could not help but notice the quick banter and newfound engagement between James Knox and his wife.

How pleased he was in knowing they had survived the greatest crisis of their lives—the loss of their two children. And how proud he was to have been a small part of bringing them back together.

"Perhaps we will need to advertise for a new overseer's assistant," he teased, "since there is little doubt that a move to the palace by the current one is imminent."

"Oh, dear, Mr. Harding," Miriam laughed. "As if there would ever be another place on this earth than *Lavender Blue* for my James and me."

"Words from one I hold in the highest regard," Daniel replied.

CHAPTER SIXTY-SIX
LETTER FROM SVEN'S CROSSING

As James and Miriam Knox and Daniel worked steadily to re-store *Lavender Blue*, Emma worked equally hard to progress in her recovery at the sanatorium.

Although Daniel had kept her apprised of progress at the estate, they seldom discussed their life at *Arctic White* anymore, making it a welcome surprise to receive a letter from Sven Bjorstad right before Christmas 1935.

Aside from annual Christmas cards filled with each year's limited overview and greeting, nearly two years had passed since Daniel and Emma had received any real communication from anyone at *Sven's Crossing*—not that they could claim to have been any more diligent than their friends in maintaining communication.

Rudy and Helen had done the most to maintain contact by sending birthday greetings and news about their growing family, but had said little else about life north of Skagway, Alaska, so it was with profound interest that Daniel brought the letter from Sven that had arrived in the day's mail to the sanatorium to read to Emma.

After their dinner together, and then her evening treatment of breathing therapies, chest percussion, drainage-promoting inversion, and inhalation of vapors of eucalyptus, Emma swallowed her evening dose of cod liver oil before leaning comfortably against the pillow in her freshly fluffed bed as Daniel began to read.

The letter was long—six pages on both sides, written in the flowing penmanship of Sven Bjorstad. It detailed events at *Sven's Crossing*, including last winter's snowshoe hare population explosion and this year's increase in lynx sightings.

There were at least two pages detailing some medical issues faced by both Sven and Daria, reporting they had both worked through them, were feeling healthy and fit, and were grateful to no longer have to travel to Skagway for treatment.

After Daniel had been reading for a while, a nurse brought tea and honey for him along with Emma's usual bedtime snack. The welcoming brew warmed his throat, giving him respite from the arduous task of reading such a long letter out loud.

"This bit of honey in my tea has helped my throat immensely," he told Emma, before beginning to read again.

. . . and to say that Helen and Rudy have done wonders with their place would be an understatement. Not only has their church grown large enough to justify a large addition, but they have also added a school for their own five children and the children of two neighboring villages.

Of course, the big news is that their eldest child—the one married at their church two long years ago, is finally pregnant and due to give birth this summer, making Helen and Rudy grandparents!

The entire family and sometimes Daria and myself have assisted with travel into Skagway for her to see the doctor, who visits from Fairbanks. As you can imagine, this has been somewhat tedious for a woman so close to confinement, which leads me to reveal the other big news—that being that Helen and Daria have together been able to locate a teacher and her doctor husband to consider an assignment with Indian Health Services right here in Sven's Crossing!

Who could ever have imagined such an assignment would be possible? But with Helen's and Daria's persistent efforts and Helen's diligence in promoting education and health care for her own growing family and those in neighboring villages, the decision makers have come to listen and final preparations are underway to bring the couple here. They are expected to arrive in early spring 1937—little more than one short year away, and although it will be too late for Helen's daughter's birthing day, it does give bright hope to all of us here for the future.

As I know I have droned on for far longer than you might appreciate, I will close by saying that you are missed here at Sven's Crossing *and we all long for the day when you can return.*

Until then, Daria has been diligent in maintaining Arctic White, *which stands ready for your future return. As you have given no indication that such a return is imminent, please excuse my temerity as I ask you to consider allowing us to rent* Arctic White *to our new family for the period of one year or until your own return.*

With apologies for the long delays in correspondence, I remain always your faithful friend.

On behalf of myself and my Daria,
Sven Bjorstad

"We have been gone much longer than seems possible," Daniel said, as he watched Emma close her eyes in sleep. "How quickly the years pass by."

CHAPTER SIXTY-SEVEN

RESEARCH

"By this time next year, I should like to discharge you to your home," Dr. Smithson told Emma. "Although we are years, and perhaps as much as a decade away from performing clinical trials on humans, there is promising research being done on several drugs that may well be the cure for tuberculosis."

Emma blinked and then blinked again three times in succession. Nothing before this conversation had ever given her even a glimmer of hope for a complete cure.

"But there is much preliminary work that needs to be done with documenting the progress of those currently afflicted with the disease," Dr. Smithson continued. "Much like the BCG vaccine that we administered to your husband prior to your arrival here, these new drugs hold the promise that one day mankind will be free of this disease."

"How does all this affect my own care here?" Emma asked.

"Since your arrival at the sanatorium, I have been carefully documenting all aspects of your care and your responses to treatment. This has included careful assessment of any and all laboratory data, as well as the series of X-rays we have performed to assess your progress."

"I see," Emma nodded.

"Although you have done incredibly well with long remissions of this disease and enjoyed a better than average response to current therapies, at this point in your treatment we would currently be considering inserting paraffin or oil into your chest cavity to collapse your right lung—the one most severely affected—and allow it to rest."

"Does my husband know of this?" Emma said, her voice beginning to tremble.

"Last evening while you were undergoing your routine therapies, we had a lengthy discussion about the current status of your care. In view of the fact that he is in the process of restoring your home to a state suitable for recovery, as well as in anticipation of the breaking technology that is currently underway, it was our mutual agreement that you would best be served by foregoing any type of invasive procedure and instead, continue with your current regimen of rest and external interventions."

Emma felt tears welling up in her eyes at the thought of such a discussion occurring out of her presence. Although it was true that a woman's husband was responsible for all of her debt and thus, most important decisions, Daniel and she had always shared communication about decisions that affected one or both of them.

Sensing her distress, Dr. Smithson continued.

"Your husband, Mr. Harding, was very clear in informing me that no decisions would be made until he had returned today to discuss our conversation with you. However, being as I will need to be away for the next fortnight, I deemed it my personal obligation to allow you to hear all of this from my own mouth."

After several long seconds of thought, Emma looked squarely at Dr. Smithson and replied, "When Daniel—my husband—arrives, I will inform him that we have talked and instruct him to approve your treatment plan on my behalf."

"I believe you have . . . we have . . . reason to hold a great deal of hope for the future, Mrs. Harding, and when I return in two weeks, we will continue forward with our plan through the entirety of 1936, after which I will conclude my own research before moving on to another assignment.

"During that time frame, it is my desire that we can return you home in late summer or early fall, after which I will, with your permission, follow you with home visits, which will add important data to my studies."

"Thank you, Dr. Smithson," Emma said. "I feel fortunate, indeed, to be under your watchful care."

CHAPTER SIXTY-EIGHT

PROGRESS

Shortly after Dr. Smithson's departure, Daniel arrived and was immediately updated by Emma about her earlier visit with her physician.

"The news will only serve to make me work harder to prepare *Lavender Blue* for your return," Daniel said.

In truth, renovations were now nearly completed, with only the solarium to be finished when spring breezes and warmer temperatures became more conducive to the laying of the tile floor.

He and James Knox had torn out all the old carpeting and replaced it with tile, leaving only the solarium incomplete. Daniel had also ordered fine Persian rugs for each room, knowing they would provide comfort, while still being amenable to regular cleaning.

The windows had all been replaced with more modern and better insulated, not to mention much larger, additions to the home. Sunlight, after all, was thought to fight TB and in England's dreary climate, availing all sunlight was crucial. This had required that the old heavy draperies be removed, which immediately increased brightness within the home.

At night, simple wooden shutters would allow for privacy, and by day, the windows would reveal the beautiful lavender fields as well as strategically placed shrubs now planted around the house. They had even added skylights, an improvement increasingly popular in current building trends, and one that would allow Emma to feel at one with the outdoors.

By June 1936, the renovations were complete and the first harvest of lavender had been taken to market, where it had proven to be both profitable and in demand in the reemerging market for such a product.

The home of James and Miriam Knox had also undergone significant renovation, and work to restore workers' quarters was already well under way, although the use of these facilities would now be seasonal and limited to laborers temporarily transported to the area for planting and harvest.

No longer would the estate depend on resident laborers, many of whom had spent most of their lives working for and living on the estate. Tougher economic times had done away with such practices at *Lavender Blue* and elsewhere, where the streamlining of production, and in some cases automation of some services had become the new norm.

Transportation had also improved and the old Aberdonia had long ago been replaced with several modern Ford trucks, each with a large flatbed enclosed with wooden rails that made them particularly suitable for farm work.

For personal use, James Knox had selected a Ford Coupe and Daniel a Ford Roadster—each one modern in style and efficient in operation. Even Miriam had begun to drive and although she usually limited her use of the family Ford to the grounds of the estate, she had gained enough confidence to occasionally take the coupe into London, even despite her husband's reservations about a woman's ability to manage such a powerful automobile on her own.

On one such trip, she had stopped to visit Emma, who thereafter declared that she, too, would pilot an automobile on her own as soon as she was free to do so.

"Husband, beware!" she had teased Daniel. "Beware of the modern woman unrestrained."

CHAPTER SIXTY-NINE

REVELATION

Emma's discharge from the sanatorium some six months earlier than expected came as the biggest surprise in recent memory, a surprise that was almost immediately upended by the revelation that Dr. Smithson would be moving on to his new assignment by late August.

The return to *Lavender Blue* was both welcome and refreshing as Emma quickly settled into a routine of spending her days in the solarium and her evenings and nights inside, where she could watch the stars twinkle through the skylights above.

The fireplaces inside both the house and the solarium, brought welcome warmth from England's damp environment, and although the smoke they brought could have been problematic, Daniel had invested in new technology that accelerated the venting of the smoke outside.

On his first home visit to see Emma in early July, Dr. Smithson remarked about the cleanliness and healthfulness of her environment, as well as about the significant improvement he had observed in Emma's mental and physical health.

"Surely, it will be much easier for me to leave for my assignment in Alaska now that I know you are on the road to healing," he mentioned as he sat with Emma and Daniel for a visit after his examination.

"Alaska?" Daniel asked.

"Yes. A place near Skagway, to be exact," Dr. Smithson replied.

"That is where I am from," Daniel said, nearly speechless with surprise. "What takes you to Skagway?"

"Charmaine and I have been made aware of the need for both a physician and a teacher in the area," he replied. "And since I was born there and lived there until the age of five or six, I am anxious to return to the place of my roots—especially knowing there is a strong need for the services we can provide."

Daniel stood and walked to the window as he tried to absorb this news, before sitting down across from Dr. Smithson again.

"With all due respect, Doctor Smithson, I spent much of my life in Skagway, and I do not recall ever meeting anyone with the last name of Smithson. Emma, you've said nothing. Perhaps you know of the Smithson family?"

Emma shook her head.

"Perhaps that is because I was not known by that name then," Dr. Smithson said.

Both Emma and Daniel watched as Dr. Smithson shifted in his chair.

"It is not normally my habit to become overly familiar with my patients," Dr. Smithson continued, "but in view of the fact that I will be leaving soon and have also come to love you both as not only patients, but as persons close to my heart, I will break with personal conviction and share with you my story."

Emma and Daniel listened as Dr. Smithson told of his early life in Skagway, of how his mother had died during childbirth and of how his father had lovingly raised him alone, always seeking, but never finding a suitable mate to help raise him.

It was only when he relayed the story of his father's despondency and suicide when he was only a young boy of five that Emma put it all together.

"And if I may ask, what was your father's name?" she said in a voice so soft it was barely audible.

"His name was Derrkstad, Hans Derrkstad," Dr. Smithson replied. "Is it possible that you knew him or the woman they sent me to live with named Chan Yang?"

Emma gasped and felt faint, prompting Daniel to rush to bring her a glass of spirits.

"You seem somewhat familiar with my story," Dr. Smithson continued. "Did you know my father? It is only after I was adopted that I took on my new family's name of Smithson."

Emma could barely contain her emotion.

"I must ask you, doctor, are you then Lars Derrkstad?"

"I am indeed," Dr. Smithson replied.

"And I am Emma, the woman who worked at your father's mercantile and for whom he carried serious affection before my sudden departure to England and right before his own tragic demise."

"May I join you in the partaking of some spirits," the doctor replied. "For as much a surprise this information is to you, it is of equal surprise to me."

Chapter Seventy
Lars's Story

Lars Derrkstad Smithson, MD paced the floor of Emma's solarium, a look of frank disbelief coupled with wondrous joy on his face.

"How often I've thought of you over the years," he said, "and yet you were right here under my very own care and I did not recognize you."

"But you were only a child when we last saw each other, and I, well, I was much younger myself," Emma said gently.

"Charmaine, my wife, sings the song you taught me to her students. I've never forgotten it," he said.

So, it had not been the drugs or hallucinations that had made her think she was hearing that song while in the solarium.

"I heard her sing, yet I did not realize it was real," Emma said simply.

"You were heavily sedated in order to promote rest and healing," Lars said, "and as for myself, I was so determined to administer the finest care that I failed to allow myself to see you as more than just another patient. Of, course, there was the name change, and the difference in locale, and . . ."

"So, it is you and your wife who will be the new doctor and teacher at *Sven's Crossing?*" Daniel asked.

"Yes," Lars replied. "Have you been there?"

Emotion washed over Emma once again as she explained how Lars's father had built a beautiful cabin for his wife before she died, and had left it to her in his will.

"It's because of your father and his love for your mother that I found myself in *Sven's Crossing* at all—that and the fact that after her husband died, Chan Yang became a decidedly different person, forcing me to find new living arrangements when few were available in Skagway at the time.

"I do not remember her fondly," Lars said, his brow furrowed. "She used to beat me for small things she found me doing wrong—like folding the clothes in the laundry the wrong way."

"She beat you?" Emma moaned. "Oh, how sad that makes me feel. I must tell you that after I left I came back for you. My plan was to adopt you as I had heard rumors of mistreatment by Chan Yang and other rumors that you had begun falling by the wayside and engaging in thievery and other mischief."

"After I had run away the last time, Chan Yang began to ask people in Skagway for help. Somehow, my father's cousin, Paul Smithson, learned of my plight and agreed to take me in. He was a doctor himself and he and his wife saw to it that I received a good education, which guided me toward medical school.

"Although of stern demeanor, he was as good a man as his wife, Anne, was sweet. They became my parents and I loved them as they loved me. Sadly, they are both gone now, leaving me—except for my Charmaine— once again alone."

Emma wiped away tears as she listened and then explained to Lars how she had come back, moved into the cabin his father had built for his mother, and had met and married Daniel once he had come to terms with his own devastating loss.

"And so, because of my father, you met Daniel and he became healed and you each found love for each other?" Lars asked. "And because of Yun and Chan Yang you found healing and shelter until you and Daniel's destinies could intertwine?"

Lars wiped tears from his own eyes as he spoke.

"I remember my father as a caring and a lonely man, and as we have been talking, I am recalling mental glimpses of the look in his eyes when you were around," Lars said. "My father would have loved knowing that because of him, you and Mr. Harding found love with each other. He would have wanted for you what he could not find for himself, of this I am certain, Miss Emma."

CHAPTER SEVENTY-ONE
NEW ADVENTURES

With Emma thriving in her post sanatorium life at *Lavender Blue*, she felt strong enough to join Daniel in driving Lars and Charmaine to the freighter terminal in Southampton.

During the drive, they learned that Lars would be continuing his research on Tuberculosis from *Sven's Crossing* by increasing the study of Native Alaskans, many of whom were afflicted with the disease.

"The school built by Mr. and Mrs. Munson will provide a convenient location from which to expand my studies," Lars told them, "and a location where Charmaine can begin to develop the educational opportunities for the area."

Emma closed her eyes as she felt the fresh air from the open car window wash across her face. Could she ever have imagined back when she first fled Hershell's bed for Alaska that now, nearing the age of sixty-three, she would be bringing her life in Alaska to full circle?

She felt Daniel's hand over hers as he leaned away from the steering wheel to ask in a barely audible whisper if she was okay. Using a system of silent communication they had perfected years ago, three gentle squeezes back told him she was.

"We are so grateful for your generosity in allowing us the use of your cabin until we can build our own," Charmaine said from the rear seat of the roadster.

Emma nodded and smiled. It was fitting that Lars and his wife would use the cabin. Although Hans Derrkstad had bequeathed it to her, if he were now alive, surely, he would agree.

"We are scheduled to reach Skagway in early September and consider ourselves fortunate that we have been able to secure passage at all, with talk of the Second World War limiting the use of many ships for public transport in order to ready them for a possible war effort. With strong hope that war can be averted, we press on."

Indeed, talk of a second world war had begun, a thought that sent shudders through Daniel in fear that *Lavender Blue* would again be caught up in reverses brought on by matters out of his control. The current world unrest was palpable with most clinging to the hope diplomacy would prevail.

"Please, if it is not an imposition, in these unsettled times would you consider telegraphing news of your arrival so that we may rest assured that you have arrived safely?" Emma asked Lars.

"It will be our honor and duty to honor such a request," Lars answered, as he helped Daniel carry his and Charmaine's bags to the baggage area.

"We hope to see you both in *Sven's Crossing* one day," Charmaine called down from the passenger deck as the steamship pulled away from the dock.

"Stay well, Emma. Daniel." Lars called to them.

"Bon voyage," Emma whispered as she squeezed Daniel's hand.

Daniel squeezed back and held Emma's hand firmly within his own. If there was a way, he would take Emma back to *Arctic White,* and if anyone could find a way it was he.

So as not to tire Emma, the two stayed in a hotel in London for the night before resuming travel back to *Lavender Blue* the next morning. By the time they arrived, Daniel had already begun seriously considering the potential of their return to *Sven's Crossing* as soon as next summer. With Emma's doctor there, surely if she could endure the lengthy trip, their life in Alaska could resume.

Meanwhile, he would talk with Emma soon about transferring control of *Lavender Blue* back to James Knox—control he had temporarily removed during the difficult times the family had undergone.

"I feel such hope that our life will be normal again soon," he told Emma. "Surely we've sacrificed enough time in suffering to deserve happiness once again."

"The suffering has only made us stronger," Emma said, "And brought us closer."

"So it has," Daniel answered. "So it has."

CHAPTER SEVENTY-TWO
THE CIRCLE OF LIFE

The telegram arriving in mid-September was welcome news to Emma, Daniel, and the staff they shared it with at the sanatorium on their next trip into London.

SAFE ARRIVAL. BEAUTIFUL. FEELING LOVED. LARS AND CHARMAINE

With *Lavender Blue* now fully functional and profitable again, Daniel had taken steps to returned full control to James Knox, leaving himself available only for consultation when asked. For his part, James Knox continued his lifetime practice of keeping them apprised of operations, one of the traits Daniel liked most about him.

Miriam's relationship with the Queen Mother continued to flourish as she enjoyed premier status as a direct consultant to the monarchy. Unlike in days past, she held little reservation about driving to London alone, although the palace usually sent a chauffeured limousine to transport her to London. Still, her main interest was helping her husband maintain the quality of operation they had always strived for at the estate, and as honored as she was to be recognized by the Palace, she continued to consider maintaining *Lavender Blue* her most loved undertaking.

Emma continued to improve as well, receiving monthly visits from a colleague of Dr. Smithson's, who forwarded details of her status to him in Alaska.

Three letters arriving at Christmas all confirmed that life at *Arctic White* was flourishing.

. . . our daughter's baby is now a healthy 3 months of age and despite her difficult birth, our daughter is serving as an assistant at the school to the very wonderful Charmaine Derrkstad Smithson.

Rudy and I miss you terribly and feel like life will not truly be complete at Sven's Crossing *until you can both return.*

God's Eternal Love,
Helen and Rudy

***

. . . the new doctor and his wife are fully enjoying Arctic White, just as they continually express gratitude at your generosity in allowing them to live there. We have only recently—and amazingly—come to learn that Dr. Smithson is the son of Hans Derrkstad, he having told this to Rudy Munson and Rudy to us.

With love from Daria and myself.
Sven Bjorstad

***

. . . how privileged we feel to be living in the very cottage my father built for my mother and later bequeathed to you! Every loving detail is as evident now as it was when he built it. Arctic White *is indeed a testament to my father's great love for my mother and for you, Miss Emma.*

And Charmaine has often expressed how at home she feels in Sven's Crossing *and has blessed me this Christmas with the news that she is with child, with her expected date of confinement estimated to be mid-May of the coming year.*

With our Deepest Gratitude and Affection for you both
Lars and Charmaine

"The news from *Sven's Crossing* has prompted me to investigate the possibility of our returning there in the coming spring," Daniel told

Emma over breakfast one morning in late December. "As we turn the calendar into the new year of 1937, with your permission I will pursue travel arrangements for late spring."

"It would be my greatest wish to return there," Emma answered. "A return I once thought would never be possible again."

CHAPTER SEVENTY-THREE

NEW YORK

Emma and Daniel arrived in Germany on May 1, 1937, having decided to forgo the coronation of King George VI and Queen Elizabeth scheduled for a little more than a week later, and despite the fact that Miriam had offered them preferred seating due to her affiliation with the monarchy. Instead, they had chosen to undertake a new adventure and be among the first to fly to America aboard a new trans-Atlantic passenger aircraft called a zeppelin.

They had been planning the trip since Valentine's Day when Daniel had presented Emma with two tickets for travel in early May.

"It's been so long since we've traveled and you deserve only the finest," he had told her, and so through skillful negotiation, he had secured the tickets for the first of ten scheduled cross-Atlantic round-trip flights between Europe and America, this one originating in Germany and scheduled to return in time for the coronation. Unlike many, however, they would not immediately return, but would travel to New York, Seattle, and then on to Skagway, Alaska, where their friends in *Sven's Crossing* were already planning for their arrival.

"It will be such an adventure, Daniel," Emma had enthusiastically replied upon receiving the tickets. "We'll be the envy of everyone we know!"

Preparations prior to the trip had been intense, with several meetings with their attorney having been completed in order to ensure that affairs at *Lavender Blue* would be able to withstand their prolonged absence.

As they had done before previous travels, they had reviewed all their papers and contracts, including updates for contingencies should they meet with long delays or ill fortune.

The trans-Atlantic flight would take three days, after which they would spend a week in New York so that Daniel could engage his business interests there. Then, as they had done so many times before, they would travel by rail to Seattle and board a steamship to Skagway, with an expected arrival on June 6.

. . . We can hardly contain our excitement here in Sven's Crossing, Sven had written on hearing the news, assuring them that *Arctic White* would be vacant as construction on the home being built by Lars and Charmaine was expected to be completed by then.

And, so, just prior to boarding the dirigible, *Hindenburg* on May 3, 1937, they sent a telegram to Sven Bjorstad:

WILL ARRIVE LAKEHURST ANS, NJ MAY 6, TRAVEL NY CITY SAME DAY, TRAIN TO SEATTLE MAY 14. ~ DANIEL HARDING.

News of the several thunderstorms in the New York/New Jersey area that day did not reach Sven Bjorstad or the others in *Sven's Crossing,* as national and even international news in those days was subjugated by the more important news of Alaska's own issues.

Neither then, despite massive international coverage, did the news about the fiery explosion of the *Hindenburg* upon attempting to dock at Lakehurst, or the loss of untold numbers of passengers and crew during this unprecedented disaster reach them.

Instead, as the people of *Sven's Crossing* gathered near the railroad tracks on May 14, 1937 to greet their friends Emma and Daniel Harding, they were greeted by one of the railroad officials who frequented the small enclave, who presented them with several newspapers highlighting the disaster and a telegram that had been sent to the railroad office notifying officials that Daniel and Emma Harding were believed to have perished in the crash of the *Hindenburg* and would not be keeping their reservation from Skagway to *Sven's Crossing.*

As if in slow motion, the group had returned to *Sven's Crossing* burdened in sorrow as celebrations for the couple's return were cancelled and replaced by a state of deep mourning that overtook all who lived there.

"It is with the deepest sorrow and with untenable regret that I ask our Heavenly Father to look after our friends, Emma and Daniel Harding in heaven," Rudolph Munson read from a speech he had written himself at a special memorial service on June 21, 1937. "It is one of life's true ironies that I am able to read this blessing aloud after writing it in my own hand only due to the diligence and kindness of Emma Brownston Harding, who took the time and interest in me many years ago to teach me the needed skills to so present these words to you today."

Tributes by the others followed, with Helen reading several of Emma's favorite works by Robert Service, and Sven and Daria telling tales of the time that Emma had gone out into the intense winter cold only to be nearly killed by Daniel, with no one ever imagining then that the two would one day find love.

But it was Lars Derrkstad Smithson who summed things up the best.

"As I walk on the lavender-flowered rug in the main room at *Arctic White*, I see Emma and her beloved *Lavender Blue*. As I traverse the rugged path from the main house to the old cabin over the rise, I see her beloved Daniel, and as the sun rises, and the rain falls in lilting melody, I hear Miss Emma singing to me as a child:

One plus two
Plus three plus four
Makes for ten
Let's count some more

Four minus two
Makes two again
Add three for five
My smart young man

And I know soon I will hear my own child singing the same song as taught by my own beloved wife, giving me assurance that Emma Brownston Harding will always remain within my heart, just as she remained within the heart of my father and will remain in the hearts of each of you here today."

CHAPTER SEVENTY-FOUR
JUNE 21, 1947

Lars watched his daughter trying to teach her younger brother to walk on the lavender-flowered carpet in front of the fireplace at *Arctic White*. He and Charmaine had long ago decided to remain in *Sven's Crossing*, having stopped construction on their own home in order to accept the bequeathment of *Arctic White* to their family.

"Emma," he called to the young girl they had named after the woman who had so profoundly influenced his life. "Gather up little Hans, I heard your mother calling."

There had been no hesitation in naming their first son after Lars's father, allowing the names of his children to carry the memory of each of those so important to him, to live on. One day *Arctic White* would belong to them and by that time they would have learned of the special legacy that had been placed into their hands.

James and Miriam Knox would be arriving soon from England on their second visit to Alaska—the first having been on the one-year anniversary of the death of their friends, after James Knox had written to Lars that they would feel much closure at the loss of their beloved estate owners if they could meet their Alaska friends and see snippets of the life Emma and Daniel had so loved in *Sven's Crossing*.

It was Sven and Daria who met them at the train, having brought along a buggy to take them to *Arctic White*.

"We have each read and reread the journal Emma so meticulously kept," James Knox said as they approached the cabin. "And just as before, we can easily see the beauty that drew our Emma here. Perhaps on this return trip we will be fortunate enough to also see one of the wilderness animals she so often referenced in both her letters and her diary."

Sven laughed at the formality of James Knox's speech pattern, before secretly vowing that if it were within his power, wild animals would surely present themselves soon.

The Knoxes, being somewhat older than the Smithsons, took immediately to the children, engaging them as they might have their own grandchildren if their sons had not perished in the war.

"Despite having built a large addition, we have preserved the main house at *Lavender Blue* in memory of Emma and Daniel," he said. "Its use will be at your disposal as our family welcomes you to Alaska."

By the time they had put their bags away and freshened up, it was time to make the trek to the home of Rudy and Helen, where tables had already been set up and a service planned to honor the couple who had brought them all together.

As they walked the trail up the rise above the Munson's homestead, a sudden rustle in the brush startled James Knox as he quickly moved in front of Miriam despite his own fears of what might have caused the disturbance.

"At this point we should remain quiet," Sven Bjorstad said, as he raised the shotgun from his hip and moved ahead of the others.

He had gone only about 100 feet when he saw a sow grizzly with two very young cubs walking along a creek bed. Motioning for the others to follow, he took them behind a rise and watched as the bear moved along the water's edge, stopping long enough for a drink and then rolling onto her back to nurse her cubs.

For the next hour, the members of the group stood transfixed, watching this normally unseen moment in nature. Even the children remained still, allowing the bear to feed her young uninterrupted.

Once the bears had moved on, the group continued on to the Munson homestead, where they were greeted on arrival by expressions of mixed concern and relief.

"We will long treasure this most special of days," James Knox said, as the group gathered for dinner and then an evening of telling stories about each of their lives with Emma and Daniel Harding—an evening that included select readings from Emma's journal.

And so as the sun barely dimmed on this longest day of the summer and the tenth anniversary of the loss of their friends, those gathered celebrated the friendships born from each of their personal encounters with Emma Brownston Harding and the man named Daniel who had brought her true love.

Today and forever, those gathered at this moment in *Sven's Crossing* would remember *Lavender Blue* and *Arctic White* through the stories of love, struggle, and hope that one woman from Britain brought to their lives as she lived *Her Story*.

www.ingramcontent.com/pod-product-compliance
Lightning Source LLC
Chambersburg PA
CBHW051648260626
47170CB00004B/1397